3/17

a novel by

Mary Pat Hyland

Also by Mary Pat Hyland
The Cyber Miracles (2008)
A Sudden Gift of Fate ~ the sequel to The Cyber Miracles (2009)

© Mary Pat Hyland
All rights reserved.

This book may not be reproduced, in whole or in part, in any form (manual or digital), without permission of the author.

This book is a work of fiction. The names, characters, location and plot are the creation of the author and should not be considered real. Although inspired by real life experiences, the characters in this novel (except for the public figures whose part in the story line is entirely fictional) do not exist and any resemblance to persons living or dead is unintentional and coincidental.

First edition
September 2010
Printed in the United States of America
Set in Georgia typeface

Cover design by Jocelyn Bailey
Cover photograph by Mary Pat Hyland

Official blog: 317thenovel.wordpress.com
Author's official web site: marypathyland.com

For Brian & Peggy Hyland
in fond remembrance of surviving
3/17 performances past.

With deepest gratitude to:
- my editors: Anne, Sheila, Brian, Kate, Dáithí & Patty;
- cover designer Jocelyn Bailey;
- Ingrid, for location logistics;
- Comhaltas Ceoltoirí Éireann for keeping the path of true Irish music alive;
- And to Liz, LunaJoon and the Triple Cities Writers Group for their encouragement and inspiration.

The first draft of this novel was completed during
National Novel Writing Month (November 2009),
a great platform for the encouragement of
putting your stories on paper.
Learn more at www.nanowrimo.org.

~ With apologies to Dante Alighieri ~

Author's note:
For pronunciations of the main characters' names and translations of the Irish language and slang used in this novel, see the lexicon at the back of the book.

PROLOGUE

Fionn MacConnell slouched in a salvaged confessional booth at the back of a Galway pub called The Vestibule, staring at his untouched pint of Guinness and a shredded photograph of his ex-girlfriend, Renny. It was half nine in the morning.

Fists curled tightly, he closed his eyes and saw her there in the pub again, just hours earlier, fingernails digging into her Amy Winehouse beehive as she screamed a litany of reasons why their relationship was damned:

"Ye culchie-brained, lazy-arsed, busker-poor eejit! Ye're never gonna be famous. Ye haven't a feckin' clue where yer goin'!"

It wasn't so much her insults that stung him—he'd been called far worse—but the fact that her meltdown interrupted a brilliant session that included his mates and some well-known traditional Irish musicians. Jaysus, it was mortifying! Of course, when you factored in Fionn's legendary temper, their hostilities erupted into a war of words on the scale of the Battle of Clontarf. (He, of course, represented the Brian Boru side, she—the bloody Vikings.)

Fionn knew by now the tale of this epic breakup was already out there, growing in scale with each kilometer it traveled down the *bótharín* from the pub. He could imagine the other musicians' whispers in the distance: "Remember that poor lad who came in second at the All-Ireland fiddle a *cúpla* years back? Och the eejit, got into a terrible row with his girl. She was after a few pints and created such a commotion! Wanted him to compliment her new dress, but he was in the middle of playin' the 'Maid Behind the Bar.' Well, the evil she-wolf flew into jealous rage, jumped up on a table and started throwin' things, left and right. Breakin' pint glasses and mirrors, cursin' Our Lord. Disgustin'! Took three patrol cars of gardaí to break up the fisticuffs that followed! Feckin' brilliant. Ye shoulda seen it!"

Fionn sank his head into his hands. Och, how could he have been codded again so easily by a girl? 'Twas yet another bleak chapter in the endless tome of his doomed love life.

They'd met on a warm May afternoon, when he was out walking to clear the peaty fog of last night's Guinnesses from his brain. He'd wandered by the Spanish Arch and saw Renny in the distance feeding a cluster of swans along the River Corrib. A slight wind teased her towering mane of jet black hair. He was riveted by the sight. When bay breezes lifted her skirt, displaying red fishnet stockings above thigh-high boots, he was overcome by zombie-like lust and marched toward her craving a carnal carnival ride.

He got one, all right. Several months into their tempestuous romance, they tried to make it about more than just sex. She'd even asked him to teach her how to play the *bodhrán* so she could be part of The Vestibule's weekly sessions. After two "lessons," it was obvious that every bit of rhythm she had in her was best used for something else. The problem was, the more he lingered with her, the less time he spent at his music—an important part of his income and the very heart of his soul. He could no longer afford this love drug, but she was a devil of a habit to break.

After Renny solved that problem by dumping him so publicly last night, he took his pint and crawled into the old confessional booth. The only light within came from a Sacred Heart votive candle that Fionn watched flicker from moonset to sunrise. The publican, an old family friend, locked up and kindly left him inside to collect his thoughts and pride.

Fionn stuck his right thumb into his mouth and nibbled on the fingernail. It was a childhood habit inspired by his namesake, Fionn Mac Cumhaill. The legend goes that young Fionn burned his thumb cooking the salmon of knowledge for the druid poet Finn Eces. When he sucked on his blistered thumb to cool it, he swallowed some of the salmon's skin stuck to it and received the knowledge of all things, a gift he later used to defeat his adversaries.

Fionn MacConnell ached for such a gift at the moment. What the feck do I do now, he worried. He chewed his fingernail a bit more. That's it! Fionn flipped open his cell phone and called his cousin Des in the States. After six rings, it picked up.

"Hallo?"

"Des. It's me."

"Whaaa?"

"Me, yer cousin Fionn." Fumbling and crashing noises filled the background for a few seconds.

"Fionn, ye feckin' eejit. It's feckin' four in the mornin'."

"Sorry, lad. It's just that ... Des ye've gotta help me. I gotta get outta here."

"Gardaí after ye?"

"No. Worse. Me girl dumped me in front of the Tuesday night session."

"Och. Ye poor lad. That's bleedin' awful." Des rubbed his eyes and yawned.

"I know. The whole feckin' pub was watchin', too. All these trad legends were there, Johnny Pat Derrane, Micko Harnett and even Tommy Kilcooley. Me reputation's completely banjaxed."

Des snickered.

"That Renny's mental, I tell ye. The craic was so mighty, the music even better. Then she went and spoilt it."

"Didn't I warn ye about stayin' away from them Claddagh swans? I told ye, they's enchanted."

"I know, Des. I know. And boy, she's some witch all right! A talented witch, but she's a feckin' mental one. Can ye help me lad? I'm dyin' here. Need a reason to get out of this place."

Des yawned as he tried to come up with a suitable scheme to help his cousin.

"This is what ye what yer gonna do. Get yer trad band back together and we'll get ye over here in March for a tour of the States."

"A tour of the States, with me band? Brilliant! Och, I'm lovin' the sound of this, Des. I'm not leavin' to save face, I'm leavin' 'cause me American fans are pinin' for me."

"Ye know, Fionn. It'll be easy money, too. Yanks love nothing better than a good piss-up before St. Patrick's Day. They start celebratin' six months to a year before. No word of a lie. Me friend Sean booked a few indie bands at some college campuses in upstate New York last fall. I'll see if he can book yez a tour."

Fionn hung up and smiled. He'd lost his girl and gained

some gigs. Interesting 24 hours, he thought. This working trip—his first to America—would be atonement for his recent sins. He'd no longer take his musical gift for granted. He'd share the gospel of traditional Irish music with the new world.

"All I have to do now is put a dacent band together." Fionn emptied his pint, blessed himself and exited the confessional booth.

FÁINNE #1

As he took Exit 9 South off Interstate 81, Fionn remembered for a serendipitous moment that Dante Aligheiri imagined there were nine circles of hell. He wondered if he was headed for the first circle ahead as a hellish snow squall churned toward the car, extinguishing the glare of sunlight above.

His bandmates—Diarmuid, Peadar and Aisling—were with him, trying to sleep off last night's fun during the endless, bumpy drive from Boston to upstate New York. Fionn wished he could take a nap, too. Here it was Thursday already of their first week in America, and he was totally knackered from the late nights spent with Des and the band.

Ramp pavement rumbled under the tires as Fionn strayed onto the ridged shoulder. He jerked the steering wheel suddenly to the left, startling the others in time to see the approaching whiteout. "Mind yer speed, Fionn," Peadar said from the back seat. "The roads could turn slippy fast."

"Sorry." Fionn pushed his long black hair out of his eyes and gripped the wheel as he replayed Des's voice in his mind: *"It'll be easy money."* Hmm, Fionn wasn't convinced. So far the band had performed three less than crowded gigs in The Craic, a Southie dive that Des referred to as his office. At the last gig, they met a lone traditional Irish music fan who looked like a female Bob Marley. Unfortunately, the rainbow-haired girl was under the misguided belief that she could play the bodhrán, and her jerky rhythms kept throwing them off the beat. Shades of that evil Renny, he thought.

Fionn felt a sudden chill and shrugged his shoulders. Was he doing the right thing? Was it worth risking the lives of his bandmates on this wintry road into the unknown, just so he could save his busted ego? Besides that, Des's easy-money promise was fading faster than the sunshine behind them.

"Turn right at the end of the ramp," a disembodied voice from the dashboard said.

"Do ye think I should trust this GPS?" Fionn asked while making the turn, glancing in the rearview mirror at an empty road hugging the Tioughnioga River behind him. The squall, thicker than a Wicklow Mountains fog, veiled the road ahead quickly. They passed a barely legible sign for Kennedy State Forest. Fionn wondered if that it meant this was an area where Irish immigrants settled. Could this be a good omen? Then he remembered there happened to be a U.S. president by that name, too.

Snow swirled furiously across the windshield, limiting Fionn's view of the road. No one spoke for a few miles until the GPS broke the silence.

"Turn left onto County Route 392."

"I think this is what the Yanks call the boonies," Diarmuid said, drinking a can of Headbanger's CaffeineX as the car climbed a curvy, wooded road.

"What if the GPS could read our minds?" Aisling said from

the back seat. "What if it could sense all of our fears at this moment?"

"Is that yer inner druid talking to ye again, luv?" Peadar asked with a wink.

"Aw go on! Tell me. Wouldn't that freak ye out right now?"

The clouds parted and the temperature fell as quickly as the sun behind the steep hills. Snow froze swiftly on the shoulders of the road and Fionn felt the tires glide when the car rolled over icy patches. Des had lent them this car for their tour. He told Fionn he'd had it all checked out, but someone obviously hadn't inspected the tires thoroughly. Fionn wished he'd realized this before starting up this empty country road.

Diarmuid leaned forward to play with the buttons on the GPS. He clicked the higher elevation view to see how far they were from the college in Dryden. "Look, there's a Page Green Road coming up. Hah! Almost like it knows we're an Irish band on a pre-St. Patrick's Day tour."

"See the GPS *is* reading our minds," Aisling said as she poked Diarmuid between his shoulder blades.

"Ow! That hurt! Ye've ruined me for me guitar-playin'."

"Och! Ye've gone too far."

"Are ye talking to Fionn or Aisling?" Peadar chirped at the GPS.

"There's no turning back now, ye eejits."

"What's with this bleedin' thing gnarling at us? I'm beginning to think Aisling's right." Fionn tapped a button to return to the street elevation view on the small black dashboard screen as he steered around a long bend.

"*Púca ahead. Swerve to avoid collision.*"

Diarmuid put his face right up to the GPS. "Ha-ha, ye cheeky little minx. Ye'll not be frightenin' the likes of us."

"Fionn! Look out!" Aisling screamed. She pointed toward the front of the car as a black pony galloped across their lane. Fionn dug his foot into the brakes but the old tires had no bite on the greasy road. The car fish-tailed across the pavement, then slid down a steep culvert. Metal scraped rock, playing a cacophonous tune in the key of deep-shite major. The car lurched forward and ricocheted back with a thud.

"*Jaysus!* Everyone OK?" Fionn looked toward the back seat.

"Yeah. What the feck just happened?" Diarmuid said as he tried to open the front passenger side door.

"We nearly killed a Connemara pony to death," Peadar said. "Where'd it go?"

Aisling folded her arms tightly to stop her fright-induced shivering. "Feck's sake that GPS was right. It *was* a púca. Did yez see its glowin' eyes?"

Fionn ignored her Celtic spirit analysis and focused on the more important matter at hand. "Can anyone open their doors?"

"Not this one, Fionn," Diarmuid said.

"Mine's banjaxed, too." Peadar pounded on his door but it wouldn't budge.

"We're going to *die* here!"

"Calm down, Aisling," Fionn said. "Give it another try." She grabbed the door handle hard and luckily the door swung right open. They clambered out her door and stood in the snowy woods, their steamy breath swirling in the headlights.

"So much for our grand tour of the States," Diarmuid snickered.

"Better turn off the headlights, Fionn. Conserve the battery in case we have to sleep in there tonight."

"Yer right, Peadar." Fionn pulled the keys out of the ignition.

"Where the feck are we?"

"At the foot of a hill where the valley ended," the GPS said.

"How can that blasted thing still be speaking to us?" Fionn asked.

"It's reading our minds," Aisling said. "It's telling us we're going on a journey of some sort."

"Stop it, Aisling. Yer giving me the willies with all yer druid-speak," Peadar said as he stepped back from the car.

"Didn't ye hear it yerself, Peadar? That wasn't me speaking just now."

"Maybe it's like a Magic 8-Ball? Let's ask a question." Diarmuid stroked his goatee. "Right then, oh magical GPS, tell us how do we get out of this mess?"

Silence. Just then a flicker of headlights cut through the forest up ahead.

"We're going to be saved!" Aisling hopped up and down clapping her hands together. But the pickup truck's driver didn't notice them and roared past. Her glee tumbled into a frown. "We're going to die. Right here. Within hours. They'll have to pry our frozen bodies off this ground."

"Help is on the way."

Fionn raised his eyebrows at the others.

"Maybe we're on some prank reality show," Peadar said as

he glanced overhead at the pine branches. "Are there TV cams hidden in these trees? We could be on Power O'Toole's 'Laugh Shanty' right now." He waved (just in case).

Diarmuid snickered and walked toward the car for another look. "I'll have a sip of what yer drinkin' there, Peadar boyo."

"If that bloody thing talks to us again," Fionn said, "I'm gonna start runnin' down the hill."

Headlights flashed at them from the other direction. They saw a tow truck coming up the hill. All four of them ran to the side of the road and waved at the truck liked they were drowning, but it sailed past.

"If they don't find us fast enough, a pack of wild coyotes will eat our frozen bodies...," Aisling said, her words drifting off into the silent forest.

"Anyone have paper and pen?" Peadar asked. "I want to leave a note for me family back in Mayo." Fionn rolled his eyes.

A third time they saw headlights approach. It was the tow truck returning down the hill. This time the driver stopped when they waved.

"You folks in some trouble?" the driver yelled from his cab.

"Typical observant Yank," Diarmuid muttered. The man got out and crossed the road to their car.

"Thanks for helpin'," Fionn said. "A pony just ran across the road and I swerved to avoid it. Next thing I knew, we were in this ditch and there the pony was. Gone."

"A pony you say," the man said, giving Fionn a look as if he thought this kid might be drunk. "A big 'un?"

"Smallish, black."

"A Connemara pony, I'd say," Peadar chimed in.

"Is that so?" The man winked at Aisling as he examined the back end of the car. "Looks like you've busted the axle son. I could give you a lift into town. You'll have to wait until tomorrow to have anyone look at this. This bein' a foreign-made car, dunno if Butch has the parts. My name's Virgil by the way. Virgil Keane."

"Are ye Irish, with a name like Keane?" Peadar asked, smiling broadly.

"I'm American, but I've been told our people came from there."

"That's where we're from. We're musicians. Over here on tour," Fionn said.

"Well I'll be dipped. That so? What sort of music do y'all play?"

"Traditional Irish."

"You mean like 'Danny Boy'?"

They all looked at each other and sighed.

"Not exactly."

"Well, don't know about you all, but I'm gettin' pretty damn cold here. We can discuss this more in the truck. Let's get your car up on the bed."

They grabbed their instruments and suitcases out of the trunk, crossed the road gingerly and climbed into the roomy, rusty cab of Virgil's truck.

"Wait, forgot something," Fionn said as he went back over to the car and grabbed the GPS system, rolling up the cord and sticking it in his coat pocket. When he passed in front of the truck, he noticed its license plate was IFRN317. He chuckled. It looked like an abbreviation for the Irish word for hell, *ifreann*.

"Did yez see that creek over here?" Peadar said. "Lucky we weren't goin' downhill when that púca crossed. We might be drowned."

Fionn slid in next to Aisling and draped his arm around her so he could fit on the seat. She smelled like that perfume made from Burren wildflowers. Lovely. He took in a deep breath and she smiled at him. OK there lad, don't get started, he thought. This trip is about restorin', not further destroyin', yer reputation. She's a dacent girl that ye've known for years and besides she's dating that Eamon fella back home, he thought. He pulled back his arm.

"Ye OK there, lass?"

She nodded.

"Where are we goin' to stay tonight?" Peadar whined.

"I'm hopin' there'll be a hostel in town," Fionn said.

"We should ask yer man for directions to the best place to stay," Diarmuid said, pointing his thumb at Virgil as he approached the truck and hopped back into the cab.

"If y'all don't mind, I'm gonna come back in the daylight to get your car. It's wedged in that culvert real good. So where can I take you kids?"

"We were wondering if ye could suggest somewhere in town, fair priced lodging. Do ye know of a good hostel, or a bed and breakfast?" Fionn asked.

Virgil laughed. "Sakes, there ain't no place like that around here. That is, unless you don't mind sleepin' in a chicken coop. Heh-heh!"

The four glanced at each other, soft Appalachian banjo

music drifting across their minds.

"Listen, got an idea. Maybe you Irish kids are long lost cousins of mine. I couldn't let you sleep in a gutter somewhere. What say you stay with me and the wife tonight? Two of you can sleep in the boys' old bedroom. The other two can fight over the davenport and pullout."

Aisling's eyes widened. Why hadn't she listened to her Ma and Da and stayed at the university this semester instead of running off with these gypsy musicians? No, she was bored with her major and wanted a little adventure. Well, her wish was just granted. A road sign they passed a way back inspired the Galway newspaper headline she imagined her parents reading: "Irish band bludgeoned near Blodgett Mills."

"That'd be grand," Fionn said. "We'll compensate ye for yer troubles, of course."

Virgil laughed. "Your money's no good here, son. So you think you almost hit a black pony in the middle of the road, for real? I knew some musicians when I was a teenager, and they all smoked that funny stuff. Do you Irish smoke that funny stuff?"

"No," Diarmuid said with a straight face. "We drink it."

"Mercy! You kids sure are funny. Wait 'til my Nolene hears about the black pony. She'll think you're into witchycraft or sumpin'."

"Oh no, mister. We're Catholics," Peadar said.

"I'm Presbyterian, but I hope you won't hold that against me. Hah-hah."

They sat silently as Virgil made a U-turn, a right here, a left there, driving them even deeper into the foggy woods. Fionn had been trying to keep track of the landmarks in case he had to lead them on foot-flight away from this stranger, but with the dense fog, they could have been climbing over the peaks of Connemara's Twelve Bens and he wouldn't have known it.

Off Woodchuck Hill Road, Virgil turned onto a steep, pine tree-lined dirt road. The tow truck's springs couldn't keep up with the rock-hard ruts. Tires smacked frozen ground and the impact knocked the truck's headlights off. The band members clutched their gear and suitcases bracing for impact, but the truck slid down the grooved road in pitch darkness like coal tumbling down a chute. Peadar held his breath and began sweating profusely.

Up ahead, a lone candle glowed inside the window of a double-wide mobile home. The truck smacked another rut and the headlights kicked back on. They could see two all-terrain vehicles out in front of the home. Next to them stood a steel cage corralling two snarling black dogs, their fierce eyes glowing in the headlights.

"Wait 'til my Nolene hears I'm bringin' home a pack of Irish musicians for dinner. Sakes alive!"

Diarmuid whispered to Aisling, "He sounds like a hunter bringing home a haunch of venison to toss in the stew pot." She giggled. Virgil looked back and noted her pretty face and curly chestnut hair as he got out of the cab.

"Too bad my sons Ray and Duane aren't here to meet this filly, either. They ain't never had an Irish girl," Virgil winked to Fionn.

Aisling elbowed Diarmuid. "Och, did ye hear that? Eeuw! I feel so manky. Wish I could shower."

As soon as the band members climbed out of the tow truck,

the dogs flared their juicy gums and growled. They pawed the ground and lunged at the steel fence surrounding them, jaws opened like great whites, spiked collars clanking against metal.

Diarmuid leaned close to Aisling's ear, "Abandon all hope, ye trad musicians who enter here." His words creeped her out but there was something darkly attractive about Diarmuid's latchico looks, she thought. Of course she was attached—her boyfriend Eamon was waiting for her back home in Galway. But they weren't married or even engaged yet, right? There's no harm in a bit of checking out the competition. Peadar was already deemed out of the question. Food obsessed and probably in love with his mam, she thought. Fionn was easy on the eyes, but for all the years she knew him, he always seemed completely uninterested, all business. Maybe she'll meet an American lad she'll fancy, but defo not the spawn of Virgil, Aisling thought.

"Honey babe, look what I found at the side of the road. They're Irish, just like grandpap. Might be long-lost cousins." Nolene narrowed her eyes at the four as they came through the side doorway.

"God bless all here," Peadar announced.

Nolene patted down her fleece house frock looking for the pack of cigarettes, pulled out a lighter and lit up.

"Hope they ain't too hungry, Virg," she said as blue smoke twirled out her nostrils. "Just warming up some corned beef hash in the Crock-Pot. 'Spose I could make some deviled eggs, too."

The group examined the faux knotty pine interior of the Keane's home. There was a small table with four chairs. Bubble wrap was duct-taped to the windows as insulation from winter gales. The wrap had an amber hue from the constant smoke cloud off Nolene's unfiltered Pall Malls.

"Hi Mrs. Keane, me name's Fionn. That there's Diarmuid, next to him is Peadar and the lovely lass to his right is Aisling. We're musicians on tour of the States. Our band is called *Slí na Fírinne*. Yer husband was kind enough to rescue us after our car slid off the road near the forest."

"See tha fear in ya? Huh?"

Fionn chuckled. "The band's name means the path of truth in Gaeilge."

"Gwale gah, huh?"

"The Irish language."

Nolene picked at her teeth as her eyes squinted at the four strangers. "I thought you Irish wuz English like the rest of us." Fionn's right hand curled immediately into a gentle fist at his side.

"They said they saw a black pony in the road, up by the woods on 392," Virgil said to his wife, eyes wide as he mimed chugging a can of beer.

"Been livin' in these parts all my life, hon. Ain't never seen no black pony runnin' loose." Nolene smirked at her guests. "You kids thirsty? Would you like something to drink?"

"That'd be grand," Peadar said. "I'd love a cuppa."

Nolene snorted. "Cuppa what?"

"Tay."

"Ain't no tea drinkers in this here home, son. We have Sanka, Mountain Dew and some bottled spring water in the fridge. You don't want to be tastin' it from the tap, folks. Might be a bit risky since our well failed the E. Coli test last fall." She cough-wheezed a cloud of blue smoke that encircled the musicians. "Of course, if you're nice to Virgil, he might share a can of his precious Genny Cream Ale."

"Honey babe, do you mind if they stay the night? No place else for them to go."

"Heck, they can stay until the car's fixed. I don't mind none," she said as she gave Diarmuid a saucy look. Now *he* felt manky.

"Well, might be a while. They got one of them Korean cars. Don't know how long it will take Butch to get the part in."

Aisling nudged Diarmuid whose eyes were already wide from thoughts of an extended stay in this dwelling. Peadar cough-sneezed. He had weak lungs since his childhood, and the toxic combination of Nolene's cigarettes, dog dander and wood smoke-permeated furniture were flaring up his allergies and rosacea. Peadar's florid face alarmed Fionn.

"Lad, care to step outside with me for a minute?" he whispered to Peadar. "I'm going to ring up Des." Peadar nodded. "Excuse us for a few. We're going to get a little fresh air." Nolene frowned and stubbed out her cigarette in the sink.

"Well, I hope they enjoy the cold air," she muttered as she stirred the corned beef hash. "'Cause I ain't givin' up my coffin nails," she said, cough-wheezing again.

Once outside, Fionn opened the prepaid cell phone Des bought them. He couldn't believe that these musicians traveled to the States without one. Fionn's was somewhere under a pile of dirty laundry back at his flat. Diarmuid said he'd run out of minutes, Aisling blamed a last-minute purse switch and Peadar simply didn't see the need for one. That is, until now. The two waited for signal bars to appear on the phone with the anticipation of Boy Scouts rubbing sticks to start a fire. Nothing sparked on the phone's screen. Not even a weak half bar.

"I think them trees are chokin' the cell tower signals to yer mobile," Peadar said, looking up at the pine tree-edged darkness. "Let's wander up the road a bit."

The dogs sprung against the steel fence as they passed them again, clanging like ocean buoys.

"Even old Cú Chulainn would have feared them beasts," Peadar said, laughing as he tiptoed past.

"They wouldn't bother me that much, except they look so hungry," Fionn said.

Tree boughs creaked above as a cold wind stirred over the hilltop. Soon it billowed with strength and roared at the two men, stinging their faces with ice pellets. The road became treacherous, and their feet stumbled on the frozen, rutted mud. Finally, they reached a small clearing overhead and Fionn turned on his cell phone again. Nothing. The glow of the phone lit up their faces outlining each worry line furrowing their brows.

"Wonder if this might work," Fionn said as he pulled the GPS device from his pocket.

"Don't ye need power from the car for it to run?"

"I know, just hoped there might be some residual energy left in the blasted thing." He flicked it on but the screen remained dark. They heard howling in the distance. Aisling *was* right—coyotes were about!

"Let's get the feck out of here," Fionn said as they tried jogging back to Virgil's mobile home. Peadar's left foot hit a rut and his ankle hyper-extended.

"Shite! Me ankle's wounded!"

"Here, put yer arm around me shoulder," Fionn said. The two hobbled back as if they were running a potato sack race.

Wind outside the mobile home rattled the bubble wrap inside like maracas. Its noisy percussion rattled Aisling's nerves.

"What if they've been attacked by coyotes? How would we know?" Aisling asked Diarmuid.

"Ye've got some fertile imagination there, lass," he said, keeping a wary eye on the hostess stirring the Crock-Pot. They heard a commotion outside.

"Peadar's injured his ankle," Fionn said breathlessly as they burst open the door, the wind shoving them inside.

"Clear off the davenport, Virgil. I'll get somethin' out of the freezer to put on it." Nolene said, gesturing with a wooden spoon. Fionn and Virgil lowered Peadar onto the brown plaid sofa. Peadar winced as they lifted his legs and propped the left ankle with a pillow.

"Here ya go," she said as she draped a freezer bag filled with frosted, odd dark objects over his ankle.

"Not the turkey giblets!" Virgil frowned. "But what if they thaw out?"

"Then I'll make the stew before your birthday, that's all. Can't you see this boy's in pain?"

"Guess you're right, honey babe." Virgil frowned, adjusted his Crappie Derby cap and grabbed a Genny from the fridge.

Peadar stared at the bag containing frozen meat stubs, and the thought of what was in it nearly made him vomit. Aisling could see he was upset and patted his hand. "Hang in there, luv. We'll get ye back home to Mayo soon."

"We can hope, can't we?" Diarmuid said, smirking at the invalid.

Peadar scowled back. He thought Aisling was a sweet, lovely girl, but that Diarmuid's humor was too dark and cheeky for Peadar's taste.

"Virgil, would I be able to use yer phone to call me cousin in Boston and let him know we're OK? I'll call collect."

"Sure, you'd be able … if the darn squirrels didn't gnaw through our wires last fall. Phone company couldn't send anyone up here 'cause we've been snowed in just about ever since."

"There's no phone?" Aisling repeated to herself, eyes glazed.

"Do ye have a computer?" Diarmuid asked, then as soon as he said it, realized it wouldn't work without a phone line. He suspected the Keanes used the term wireless only in connection with bras.

"Well, folks, soup's on!" Nolene said as she lit another cigarette and let it dangle from her lips while carrying the Crock-Pot over to the table. "Maybe it's a good thing that injured boy's on the sofa. We don't have enough chairs." She cough-wheezed another blue cloud of smoke over the table as she ladled out the corned beef hash into mismatched bowls. Virgil set a loaf of white bread still in its wrapper on the table, next to the plastic tub of margarine.

"This here's a real treat for us," Virgil said as the three at the table looked down at the greasy lumps of corned beef and potato chunks in their bowls. "But I understand you Irish eat this all the time," he said as he slathered margarine over a piece of bread.

"No word of a lie," Diarmuid said, "but corned beef's never passed o'er me lips." He stared nervously at his food.

"Well, there's a first time for everything, hon," Nolene winked saucily at him as she ate her meal leaning on the counter top. Virgil raised his eyebrow. He'd have to watch that boy. Didn't appreciate his sarcasm, and really didn't like the way Nolene was taking a cotton to him.

As Peadar ate his meal on the couch, he noticed a framed picture of Calvary hanging on the wall above him. If he moved slightly, the image morphed into the risen Christ. Well, he thought, at least they have religion. Right? They wouldn't be the sort then to murder us in our sleep, right?

His eyes moved across the room to the TV set by the window. On top of it was a pewter gargoyle with red eyes that glowed from a lit candle inside it. Hmm, he wondered, maybe there's a conflict of faiths going on here? Leaning against the far wall was a particle-board bookcase with a large, dusty photo on top. It showed two young men, probably Ray and Duane, standing by a Last Supper-like display of assorted dead "trophies"—pheasants, deer, bass and a fistful of gray squirrels. Hanging above that was a velvet painting of Dale Earnhardt driving his No. 3 car through the pearly gates as St. Peter waved a checkered flag.

Hmm, Peadar mused, somethin' tells me they have catholic taste in religion. As he said a few silent Hail Marys, the wind gathered force outside and a sudden gust shoved the wall next to him.

"Feel that, y'all?" Virgil asked, corned beef dangling from the corner of his mouth. "Don't let that frighten' ya. This here home's prone to a little shake, rattle and roll when there's a good blow outside. Don't worry. We got steel bolts connectin' us to the poured concrete beneath."

Just then the wind blew so fiercely that Aisling could swear she felt the home move a couple of inches. "Does the wind rock yer home like this often?"

"Nah, just for the entire month of March. Like them tides of March I read about in school, I guess."

"We always say, if it's rockin', don't keep knockin'." Nolene patted Diarmuid's shoulder. "Say, hon, can you pass me the margarine?" Diarmuid felt Aisling kick his ankle under the table. Jaysus, she's a flirty one, he thought.

"You know what, honey babe? I think I'll take these folks over to meet cousin Brian tomorrow. He's the real Irish one in the family. You'd all like him, I bet. His three daughters do that *Riverdance* stuff. They go all the way up to Syracuse twice a week to take lessons. Bet he'd enjoy meetin' some real Irish."

Fionn smiled, but inside he grimaced at Virgil's use of the "R" word. It made him think of Renny, who told Fionn once that she had a fantasy about cutting his long locks to the length of Michael Flatley's, dyeing it a deep strawberry blond and perhaps adding a slight perm. He'd laughed at her horrifying suggestion. She whined, "But ye'd look so posh, luv."

Tryin' to change me looks—that was the first red flag about that relationship, he thought. Fionn shuddered as he shook the braying image of Renny from his mind.

"Well, thank yez all again very much for your hospitality," Fionn said. "Dinner was quite ... tasty."

"You're most welcome, hon," Nolene winked. "There's enough so we can have the leftovers with our fried eggs tomorrow."

Aisling helped Nolene clear the table as Virgil prepared the boys room for two of the guests by lifting boxes of junk and hunting gear off the beds and tossing them in his tiny office. Fionn decided to sleep on the sofa across from Peadar in case they had to flee in the middle of the night. His 6-foot-4 frame barely fit on the lumpy furniture, but he was grateful to spend the night there instead of in a freezing car. In the boys' room, Diarmuid slept in the bed closest to the door, so he could protect Aisling from intruders. She suspected that he was the one who had more to fear.

When Virgil turned off the last light, the house "disappeared" into darkness. If they held up their hands to their faces, none of the four would be able to see them. The wind cried like keening banshees as it rushed through the pines next to the mobile home. Every once in a while, they heard low growls from the dogs outside, followed by fierce barking as if a terrible row was occurring, then suddenly, utter silence.

The restless night left them exhausted when the sizzle-sputter of eggs frying in Crisco roused them early the next morning. Peadar—not quite awake—looked at his ankle, saw the bag of thawed giblets draped over it and screamed. He told Aisling later that he thought the dogs had gotten in the house and started eating his foot.

"Jayz, did I have strange dreams last night," Diarmuid said to Aisling as they sat down at the table. "I dreamed a pig was kissing me, and the pig reeked of corned beef hash." He wondered why Aisling was staring at him instead of laughing at his silly dream.

Then she took a napkin and wiped his cheek.

"What the feck are ye doin'?"

"Shh!" she whispered. "Removing pink lipstick."

"OK, who wants eggs and hash?" Nolene sang as she carried a cast iron skillet over to the table. When she put a spoon into the pan, it broke a yolk leaking thick yellow streams over the red hash. "Here you go, hon," she said to Diarmuid as she leaned in close to spoon some onto his plate. He noticed her pink lipstick.

Peadar slipped his shoes on gingerly. His ankle felt much better. The swelling was down and he could walk over to the table.

"See what a little bag of frozen giblets can do?" Nolene laughed.

FÁINNE #2

"Stopped by Brian's for a chat on my mornin' run," Virgil said as he returned while they were finishing breakfast. "Says he can't wait to meet y'all. He insists that you stay the night with his family."

"Och, that's very kind of him. I've heard yez Yanks were generous. Now I believe it," Peadar said as he finished off a corner of toast.

Virgil rubbed his hands together. "You kids ready to go fetch your car and head on over to Butch's?" They nodded, stood up to clear the table but were shooed away by Nolene.

"Run along, now. I can clean up this mess." They thanked her profusely for her hospitality and she returned the sentiment by patting Diarmuid on the behind as he walked out the door. "Don't be a stranger now," she called after him.

The band members climbed into the truck and it lumbered up the dark roads to the scene of the accident. When they got there, Virgil backed the tow truck toward the disabled car, attached some chains and then rolled it up the ramp onto the truck's flatbed.

As they waited, Aisling was trying to purge crazy thoughts of what their night would have been like if they'd stayed in the car. Diarmuid was trying to block memories of the dreadful smell of corned beef hash and the even worse taste of pink lipstick. Peadar was trying to ignore the throbbing pain in his ankle again. Fionn was wondering if Renny had noticed he was gone yet.

"How far is it to Butch's?" Fionn asked Virgil.

"'Bout eight miles up the road."

Skies cleared, the wind settled and bright sunlight melted remnants of yesterday's snow squall. Fionn took his cell phone out to see if he could get any service. He'd have to let someone know at the college that booked them that they'd probably not be make their gig tonight. Again the phone showed not even a hint of a bar. We're trapped in a cellular *Twilight Zone*, he thought.

Virgil pulled in at a rundown service station with a carved tree trunk bear waving an American flag out front.

"C'mon in Fionn, I'll introduce you to Butch."

They walked into the dirty repair shop that reeked of motor oil and stale french fries. Butch wiped his hand on an oily rag and extended it to Fionn.

"Pleased to meet ya, son. What happened to your car?"

"We came across this black pony in the road and I braked to avoid it. The road was icy, I couldn't get any traction and the car flew right into the ditch."

"They was up on 392," Virgil added.

Butch chewed gum exaggeratedly as he stared at Fionn. "Never seen a pony there, but did find a salmon in the middle of the road once. Took it home and grilled it. Darn tasty eats. Say, what kinda accent you got there, son?"

Fionn tilted his head as he wondered if Butch really said what he thought he just said. "Um . . . Irish. Mates and I have a band. We play traditional music."

Butch squinted at him and started chewing again. "You one of them IRAers? You like to blow things up, 'cause if so, we don't need no terrorists in these parts. Got enough troubles of our own, what with the phones being out from them Al-Qaida squirrels jihadin' the lines."

Fionn laughed. "No, jayz *no*! We're from the Republic of Ireland, not Northern Ireland. I promise ye, none of me mates knows anything about makin' bombs."

Butch looked past him at the three others sitting in the truck. "Guess y'all do look harmless enough. OK, I'll place an order for the parts, but this bein' one of them Korean cars, I don't expect I can get anything in before a week."

"A *week*?" There goes their gig money, Fionn thought. *Jaysus*, Aisling will freak when she hears that. And what if Peadar needs medical treatment for his ankle? Bloody hell, why did I take on this tour, he thought. Haven't I paid enough for me sins?

"We'll be in touch, Butch," Virgil said patting his oily shoulder. "Gotta go drop off these kids at my cousin Brian's."

The band saw Fionn grimace as he walked toward the truck.

"Bet it's gonna cost us our earnings," Diarmuid said.

"Don't say anything when he gets in, he probably feels bad enough," Aisling said.

"Och, why did I let yez eejits talk me into this nightmare?" Peadar frowned as he rubbed his sore ankle.

Brian Murphy's home was an aluminum-sided ranch just down the road from Butch's Zzzip-In Repair Shop. Since it was Friday morning, Brian was at work. He was the manager of an artificial insemination cooperative run by the agricultural college about 20 miles away. His wife Kelli answered the door, her hair ribbed with curlers.

"Hey, Virgil, you old dog! Brian said you were coming over." She kissed his stubbly cheek. "So are these those Irish people?" she said, tilting her head. They nodded and Diarmuid noted that somewhere in the house, The Irish Tenors were singing the theme song from *Titanic*.

"Come on in. Wait until the girls get home from school and see we have real Irish musicians staying with us," she said clapping her hands together and letting out a squeal of delight. "You know what? You can help them practice for their show at the Ruffed Grouse Lodge tonight." Diarmuid raised his eyebrow toward Fionn, who saw his reaction out of the corner of his eye but knew it was best to act like he didn't hear anything.

"So what are your names? O'He and O'She? Hah-hah-haaa."

"I'm Aisling. That's Fionn, our leader, next to ye. Diarmuid is the cute, but scary one," she giggled, "and Peadar is the gimp." Diarmuid grinned at her compliment; Peadar frowned.

"Never heard Irish names that sounded like that before. No Kevin or Maggie in your group?"

"We are who we are. Mind if I use the jacks?" Diarmuid asked.

"The wha...?"

"Yer terlet?"

She wasn't sure about this brusque "Deer-mutt" fella. He seemed a little dark. Maybe he was one of those IRA terrorists. Did she trust him using the "good" bathroom?

"You can use the one down in the rec room. That's where

you'll be staying. Follow me."

She led them down the plush carpeted stairs to a wide-open room the length of the house. They set down their instruments and suitcases and looked around the pub-sized room. One wall was filled with mirrors. There was a portable dance floor broken up into parquet squares leaning against a corner. A lighted trophy case filled with awards from Irish dance competitions lined by the far wall. Kelli led Diarmuid past it and pointed out the bathroom, whose every fixture was pink.

"This is a photo of my dancing colleens," Kelli said to the others. "That's Katie, the middle one is Kara and the youngest is Keera." The photo showed the three in their Irish dance costumes, straight bodices that flared into skirts covered with sparkly Celtic designs in garish hues. Their natural hair was covered with towering shiny ringlet wigs. They wore hard shoes with faux crystal shamrock buckles.

"That's a fine thing ye've done, introducing them to the tradition of Irish dance," Fionn said. "Did ye dance as a child?"

"No, oh no, not at all. We were shopping at the Carousel Mall in Syracuse one day and happened upon McCool's School of Irish Dance performing. The girls were interested and so I asked Kevin McCool after the show if they could sign up. We were put on a waiting list for six months before they could take a class. Kevin is from Dublin. Have you ever been there?"

"Is the pope Catholic?" Diarmuid muttered as he rejoined the group. They all laughed.

"You three fellas can stay down here tonight and Ashley can stay with the girls in their room upstairs. It will be like a slumber party," Kelli said as she gave Aisling a giggly hug. "I'll go get some sheets and blankets for you."

Aisling looked at the others and mouthed "Ashley?" They shrugged.

After Kelli disappeared upstairs, the band members got comfortable on the two couches in the rec room. Aisling fell asleep almost immediately and slumped toward Diarmuid. He put his arm around her.

"*Cailín bocht*. It looks like she's got the *coladh marbh*," he said.

"I could sleep like the dead now, too," Fionn said, stretching out on the floor so Peadar could raise his legs onto the sofa. By the time Kelli came back downstairs with the linens, they were all sound asleep.

Too soon after, the sound of tapping feet awakened them. They squinted up at three girls with springy ringleted hair standing over them.

"Mom said you were here to help us practice for the performance tonight. We need you to play a reel for 'The Blackbird,'" Katie demanded.

Fionn rubbed his eyes as Peadar yawned.

"Do yez think we could play them a number or two?" Fionn asked.

"Sure." Aisling nodded, Diarmuid shrugged and Peadar started assembling his uilleann pipes. The girls folded their arms and waited while Aisling sat up and pulled her button accordion out of its case, yawning as she slid the straps over her shoulders. Fionn tuned his fiddle and Diarmuid clamped a capo onto his guitar's fretboard. Fionn counted off and they started playing an energetic reel. The music drew Kelli downstairs. Diarmuid smirked when he read her T-shirt: "I don't dance. I finance."

"Oh, this is wonderful. Let me get the camcorder. Don't start yet girls," Kelli said as her daughters preened before the mirrors. She ran upstairs and returned just as the girls were lined up on the dance floor. "Oh, and I brought something to help the band keep time." She set a metronome on the coffee table in front of them. Diarmuid shot a look of disgust at Fionn. Aisling giggled.

"We need it at 113 beats per minute, Mom," Katie said, sounding impatient.

"After all the feises I've been to with you girls, don't you think that number is burned into my brain? Hah-hah!"

"It's *feiseanna*," Peadar said softly to Kelli, smiling sincerely at her.

"Huh?"

"The Irish word for the plural of feis is *feiseanna*."

"Mr. McCool says feises all the time and he's from Dublin," Kara said with a sneer, arms folded.

"That's because he's a fe...."

"Diarmuid, shut yer gob!" Fionn growled. "Right then, 'Miss McLeod's'?" The band sped into the reel they'd played so many times during their pre-tour practices that their instruments could play it without them. Aisling yawned again as her heavy eyes followed the glittering shamrock buckles on the girls' hard shoes. She started wondering what would be worse: freezing in the broken-down car, being eaten by coyotes or playing night after night for these feis princesses. Hmm, tough one.

Tiny Keera, arms straight at her sides, started waving fingers upward at the musicians.

"Is that little one tellin' us we're too slow?" Diarmuid muttered.

Kara did the same thing. All of a sudden Katie stopped dancing, folded her arms and frowned at the musicians.

"Listen, you're going to have to keep pace with us or else we'll just use the Paddy MacSeamus CD. *He* knows how to play for dancers."

Aisling knew that scary look on Fionn's face. She'd only seen him unable to control his anger once, and that was years ago when they were playing at a street festival in Lisdoonvarna. Paddy MacSeamus & His Dancin' Ballybunions wouldn't get off the stage when Slí na Fírinne was supposed to go on. They'd whipped the crowd into a frenzy with their campy version of a céilí dance Paddy renamed "The Sweets of Mayhem." It involved some traditional footwork, namely the sevens and threes, but included kissing and punching and ending up in an Irish-style conga line snaking around the dance floor. Since Fionn's band was the last act on stage, it angered him to see their precious time to play beautiful traditional music being wasted by this tawdry display of tourist fodder. Paddy also had an irritating habit of never quite tuning his fiddle right, which further grated on Fionn's nerves.

That day at the festival, Aisling watched Fionn's hands curl repeatedly into fists and then relax as he waited for the orange-haired Paddy to finish. The last time they curled up, they stayed that way until they connected with Paddy's jaw, knocking him to the ground and inflaming the angry dancers into a lynch mob that chased Fionn through town.

Aisling looked at the sisters and tried to decide which one Fionn was imagining punching out first. Perhaps it was their mother, who was videotaping the whole thing an arm's length away.

Fionn clutched the fiddle bow tightly, then looked at the musicians. "Faster!"

Whatever happened to dancing at the crossroads, Peadar wondered as he watched the girls in their glitter-tacky garb. He recalled dancing with his cousins back home in Mayo one sunny afternoon on a coast road by Clew Bay. Uncle Malachy played the concertina for them as they danced a four-hand reel followed by a lively Newport Set. They were wearing everyday clothes, no sparkly shamrock buckles, nary a ringlet upon the heads on his red-haired sisters and cousin Aileen. What they danced that day was far more authentic and beautiful in its simplicity, he thought, than this schlocky Vegas-style approach to Irish dance today. Even more, he noted, there's no look of enjoyment on their makeup-plastered faces. Irish dance should be simple and laughter-fueled (like that day in Mayo), not cold and driven with Olympic-like aggression. So much seemed to get lost in translation as tradition crossed the Atlantic and back.

"Girls, do your hornpipe next," Kelli said, one eye hidden behind the video camera. "You know, the one that wowed the adjudicators in Buffalo."

"Do you know how to play 'Harvest Home'?" Kara asked.

"Of course, lass," Fionn winked at her. Aisling was glad to see his inner fury had passed.

"I want 'The Mason's Apron'!" Katie pouted.

"I can only dance this to 'The Boys of Bluehill,'" Keera said, arms folded.

"If ye'd like, we can play them all and yez can take turns," Fionn said.

"I'm first then." Kara stepped forward.

"Why you? I'm the oldest. I should go first!" Katie poked her sister in the arm.

"What about me? I'm the youngest. I'm always last. Let me go first this time!"

"No, Keera!" Kara snapped. "And by the way, your elbows always bend out during competition. If you don't keep them in, you'll never place in a higher level."

"SNOT!" Keera stuck her tongue out.

Kara grabbed Keera's ringlet wig and threw it across the room. "Ha-hah, ha-hah! You can't dance without your hair!"

"*Kara!*" Kelli screeched, still videotaping. "You apologize to your little sister right this minute, missy."

"Why?"

Katie shoved Kara. "You're a brat!" Kara reached for Katie's ringlet wig, but her sister managed to pull Kara's off first. The girls kicked each other and fell to the dance floor. Keera jumped onto the pile as the girls clawed and screamed at each other.

"'The Boys of Bluehill' it is!" Fionn said. "Right then, *a haon, a dó, a haon dó trí*...." The band jaunted into a lively hornpipe as the battle royal ensued, Kelli still videotaping it all.

When Brian got home from work that evening, he noticed his girls were wearing makeup a bit heavier than usual as they ate dinner in the kitchen. He kissed each girl on the top of her head then looked around.

"Aren't those Irish people here?" he asked Kelli.

"Yes. They're eating downstairs."

"That's not very welcoming."

"Well, the girls got overly excited today during practice and there really isn't much room up here and one of them, well...," she said as she leaned in to whisper to him, "I think he might be one of those IRAs. Kinda s-p-o-o-k-y."

"We can all spell spooky, Mom," Katie said. "It's not like we're cousin Nolene."

"IRA? Really?" Brian said, raising his eyebrows toward his daughters. "Do you think it's safe for them if these characters stay the night?"

"Well the one girl, Ashley, seems very nice. She'll be staying in the room with the girls tonight."

"She's not a smoker or druggie is she? Geez, musicians can be a sordid lot. Don't want them teaching our angels bad habits." The girls beamed sweetly at their father.

"C'mon, I'll introduce you to them."

When they went downstairs, Brian saw the four eating their dinner.

"Ah, I can see Kelli's given you some of her famous corned beef and cabbage. It's always a treat for us, but I suppose you eat it all the time over there."

"Actually," Diarmuid started to speak but stopped when Aisling's elbow connected with his gut.

Fionn stood up to greet him. "Howya, Brian. I'm Fionn, the leader of the band. Can't thank ye and the missus enough for yer kind hospitality to us."

"Nice to meet you, Fionn. So who are the others?"

"Peadar, Aisling and this is Diarmuid." As Brian shook everyone's hands, Kelli nodded when he reached Diarmuid, so he'd know which one she thought was with the IRA.

"Well, this is quite a treat for us all, to have real Irish people under our roof. Have you seen the girls dance yet? I bet you think they're heading for *Riverdance*. Kelli and I are so proud of them."

The band members looked at each other, wondering who would have the courage to respond. Peadar smiled at Brian. "They're right lively dancers. Feet flyin' so fast, ye couldn't follow them." Phew, the others thought, good answer.

Brian grinned widely. "Wow, that means so much coming from pros like you. Have you ever met Michael Flatley?"

Diarmuid couldn't hold it in and snickered. "Of course! We're *very* close."

What does that mean, Brian wondered as he stared at the dark-haired fellow. Is Michael Flatley one of his IRA brethren? Oh, how would he ever be able to break the news to his innocent daughters?

"That's wonderful," Brian said carefully. "You must give our daughters a good review then. Well, gotta eat my dinner now. We'll be going to the Ruffed Grouse Lodge in an hour. OK?"

"We'll, as in all of us?" Aisling asked.

"Yes, Ashley," Kelli beamed. "Wanted to keep it a surprise, but the Grand Drummer is going to be there tonight. He leads the National Covey of Ruffed Grouse Lodges. Brian put in a good word for you and so you're the featured entertainment, after the girls dance of course."

"Lovely. Are we gettin' paid?" Peadar asked. Diarmuid smirked. Fionn scowled.

"Yes, free bed and breakfast," Brian laughed as he escorted Kelli up the stairs. When they were out of sight, he whispered to his wife, "Can't believe it! Michael Flatley ... do you suppose he's in the IRA, too?"

"Fionn, what about our gig tonight?" Aisling asked as they packed up their instruments. He took out the cell phone to see if they'd get service here. Nothing.

"Well, that answers that," Peadar said.

The band squeezed into the back seats of the Murphys' minivan and they all drove off to the Ruffed Grouse Lodge. It was a quick ride away, mercifully, and the band was led to the back of the hall where they would be setting up, right under a mammoth TV screen next to the bar. Fionn asked Kelli if the band was going to play for the girls, but she told him 'no.' The girls said they'd be less nervous if they danced to the Paddy MacSeamus CD, so all the band had to worry about was their own performance.

Fionn bit his right thumb fingernail as he walked away, thinking actually the girls and Paddy MacSeamus made a brilliant match. Peadar was explaining the uilleann pipes to the bartender when Fionn reached the band.

"*Uilleann* means elbow in Irish," Peadar said to the young man. "That's because unlike the Highland Pipes, ye know the regular bagpipes, these are played with the force of me elbow compressing the bladder here. Fingers cover the holes on the chanter to get the different notes."

"Cool. Why aren't you wearing a kilt, like the other bagpipers I've seen?"

"No need to frighten the ladies sitting across the room," Peadar laughed.

"Good man there," Diarmuid said, draping his arm around Peadar. "Right considerate, this one."

"Fionn, what's our playlist?" Aisling set down her button accordion and scooped her hair up into a clip.

"Not sure if we should start mellow or lively. Have no idea what the crowd will be like."

"Let me start with somethin' on the pipes, Fionn," Peadar interrupted. "Give them something they've probably never heard before, real Irish music!"

"Good idea there, Peadar. How about *'Táimse Im' Chodladh'*?"

"That's what I was thinkin'."

"Maybe this isn't the place fer bein' overly trad," Diarmuid argued. "Might that put this beer crowd into a deadly sleep?"

The others groaned. "What do we care?" Aisling added. "We won't be back here, *le cúnamh Dé*. Give 'em the full-blown trad, I say."

"Ye've got a point there, lass," Diarmuid said as he nodded. "One promise, no 'Sweets of Murphy Mayhem' reprise." They all laughed.

As the band tested the lodge's microphone and speaker system, members arrived and crowded the round tables scattered across the hall. The acoustics made conversations in the hall sound like they were taking place in coffee cans, and soon the band members could hardly hear each other over the escalating din. At seven o'clock the bartender locked the front door ceremoniously, then a man wearing grouse feathers closed the shades on all the windows and turned off the lights.

"What the feck's happenin'?" Diarmuid whispered.

"They're preparin' to roast and eat us," Peadar muttered out of the side of his mouth.

A flashlight beamed across the hall and landed on another man dressed in feathers. He swooped his "wings" forward a couple of times then began beating an animal-skin drum slowly. The pace quickened, sounding like a lawn mower revving up. Just as suddenly as he'd started, he stopped. Someone extinguished the flashlight and a low voice spoke from a distant corner.

"Fellow grouses, let us pause and remember the feathers that have fallen before us."

After a moment of silence the drumming started slowly again, picked up a rapid pace and stopped dead. The house lights flicked on and everyone winced.

"Good evening, loyal grouses, I'm Brian Murphy, your host for our annual St. Patty's Day Hooley."

"St. Paddy's Day," Diarmuid hissed. "He's not the patron saint of hamburgers."

"And now to get us started, a set of reels performed by those lovely lasses, the Murphy sisters—Katie, Kara and Keera. Let's give them a warm welcome!" The audience drummed on the table with their hands.

"Jaysus, will yez listen to them? It's bloody tribal," Peadar said.

"Wonder if they'll roast us on a spit or in a pit?" Diarmuid whispered. They started laughing, drawing disapproving looks from a table nearby.

The CD began playing and Fionn cringed as soon as he heard Paddy MacSeamus's untuned fiddle. It was a sound that made him want to punch his fist through the nearest window. Shatter it! He wondered if Paddy even knew how to tune his fiddle. Aisling watched Fionn's face shift from calm to angry. Ah jayz, not here, Fionn, she thought. Don't ruffle the Grouse Lodge's feathers.

Ringlets bounced, rhinestones shimmered and hard shoes snap-tapped across the linoleum floor as the Murphy girls reeled by. The faster they danced, the louder the table drumming became. Peadar's right, Diarmuid thought as he watched the spectacle. This *is* tribal.

The girls finished "The Blackbird," pointed out their right shoes and bowed. More than a few wolf whistles filled the air.

"Lovely, girls, lovely. And now, a terrific set of hornpipes for you featuring Katie first, then Kara and lastly, Keera." Paddy MacSeamus started playing "Off To California" with his fiddle off-tuned in a way that brought stale bread or a flat cola to mind. Fionn folded his arms across his chest and nibbled the nail of his right thumb, groaning at every off note as he rocked back and forth against the wall.

The tune made him think of Renny again. She'd been trying to convince him to move to California with her. They could stay with her cousin Oona who worked at a Hollywood movie theme park. Renny's grand plan? Fionn would support them by playing his music in the local bars, while she pursued her dream of becoming an actress. She'd already had a pit part in a Druid Theatre production of a Synge play. Just imagine it, she begged Fionn. Sunshine every day. Gobsmacked by all the celebs. Their posh lifestyle would be the envy of all the loser trad musicians back home.

"Posh me arse!" Fionn said aloud to no one in particular. That should have been the second red flag about Renny, he thought. "Jaysus!"

Seeing his fury build was like watching fumarole steam billow from a volcano ready to blow, Aisling thought. She looked around the room for the nearest exit should she have to make a quick escape from flying beer bottles.

"Look at her," Fionn muttered to the rest as he pointed at Katie. "She's doing the steps perfectly but missing the feel of the music totally."

"Add a few more rhinestones, luv. Ye'll blind the audience *and* every feis adjudicator. No one will notice ye've got no bleedin' feelin'," Diarmuid snickered.

"Ugh, I just don't get the fake curls and the feckin' tiaras," Aisling added.

"Aw go on, luv," Peadar said with a grin, "didn't ye want to be a princess too when yez were a little girl?"

"Princess, yes. Dancing tart, no!" They all laughed again. From across the room, Brian noticed Diarmuid's sneer and it made him nervous. He'd have to watch that IRA fella.

"How 'bout my talented colleens?" Brian beamed at the frantic drumming response. "Finally, a lovely set of slip jigs for you. My fellow grouses, once again, give it up for the Murphy sisters!"

Kelli advanced the Paddy MacSeamus CD to track six, "The Butterfly," as the audience drummed with anticipation. Again, Paddy's fiddle wove in and out of tune.

"*Jaysus*, he's bleedin' murderin' that lovely tune. And why the feck does he think he has to lilt over the music. 'Deedle-diedle-dee. Deedle-diedle-dee.' Och! I can't feckin' stand it."

"Calm down, Fionn." Aisling patted his arm, but he broke away from her. Uh-oh, she thought. Here it starts.

"That fecker ought to be drawn and quartered for all the damage he's done to traditional music. He can take his feckin' Ballybunions and shove them up his...."

"Fionn, ye look thirsty. Can I buy ye a Guinness?"

Fionn stared angrily at Peadar, then at the bar.

"Looks like all they've got here lad are bottles of piss water. About as authentic to brewing as this plastic Paddy is to Irish music."

Diarmuid tried next to get Fionn fixated on something other than Paddy's music. "Have ye tried yer mobile here? We've still got to call Des and tell him about the car."

"Yer right. I'm gonna go outside and give it a try." As he walked toward the entrance, he noticed an extension cord connected to the portable CD player on a table by Kelli. The girls were actually doing a lovely job dancing the slip jig. 'Twas a pity it would end too soon. He faked a stumble on the cord as he walked out the door and it ripped the plug out of the socket. The girls, being seasoned feis pros, continued to dance in silence while Kelli pushed buttons on the CD player frantically, trying to bring the sound back.

While Fionn tried yet again to get a signal on his phone, the ruffed grousers drummed tables loudly inside. The girls completed their routine without missing a beat and bowed to a deafening ovation.

"I feel like I'm at a death metal concert," Peadar said. "If they get any louder, I think they might disrupt me heart rhythm."

"Since when were ye ever at a death metal concert?" Diarmuid teased.

"I've been to one. With me cousin, Tommy. We saw Toss the Maggots in Mullingar."

"Sure ye did, boyo." Diarmuid patted his back and winked at Aisling.

All of a sudden Fionn got three bars on his cell phone. Yes! He was so excited, he nearly dropped the stupid thing on the ground. When he managed to ring up Des and start telling him the saga of the car, suddenly—poof—the signal vanished. He walked all over the parking lot trying to recover it, but it was no use. A rainbow would be easier to catch than a cell tower signal in this godforsaken countryside.

Fionn trudged back inside, shoulders hunched and hands in pockets, just in time to hear Brian announce there was a special treat for the audience. He raced over to the band and picked up his fiddle, ready to start into their first tune.

"Grouse cocks and hens, I'm delighted to introduce to you for the first time, singing a medley of some *real* Irish music...."

Singing? Who told him we sang, Fionn wondered.

"That beautiful lass I married, *Kelli Murphy*!"

Fionn folded the fiddle and bow across his chest as he bit his right fingernail again.

Kelli sang "My Wild Irish Rose" plaintively, hands crossed over her heart. Her ringleted hair, though odd for her age, gave her a Shirley Temple earnestness.

"Bet yez all me tour earnings that unicorn song is next," Diarmuid said, rubbing his hands together with fake glee.

"She heard ye, lad. No thanks for the suggestion." Peadar winced as the crowd started miming humpty-back camels and chimpanzees.

"So help me, if she sings 'Danny Boy'... oh nooooo ... there she goes." Aisling rubbed her brow with her hand, trying to shield her eyes from the spectacle.

"Oh no, there *he* goes," Diarmuid corrected. They gasped as Fionn walked up to Kelli, waited until she finished singing, then grabbed the microphone from her hands.

"Holy shite! That's it. We're feckin' fooked," Aisling said, cowering behind her button accordion.

"Thank yez, Kelli and the rest of the Murphy clan. They've done a fine job of whetting yer appetites for the main course tonight. Me name's Fionn MacConnell and that's me band over there. We're called Slí na Fírinne, that's Irish for the path of truth. And that's really what we are, a path to *true* Irish music. I'll be playin' the fiddle, Peadar McCloskey is that fella there on the uilleann pipes, they're like bagpipes but played with yer elbow. Next to him is Diarmuid Kinsella on guitar and the *cailín álainn* on the button accordion is Aisling Lyons. So, ladies and gents, I give yez ... the path of truth!"

Peadar played dreamily the opening notes of *"Táimse Im' Chodladh."* Its haunting melody lingered like peat smoke over the room. Fionn closed his eyes and at that moment, for the first time since they arrived in America, he felt reconnected to his homeland. He could see himself walking down the strand at Spiddal, feet dipped in Galway Bay, gazing across at County Clare and inhaling the seaweed-scented breeze. It was brilliant playing, sheer magic.

Peadar was halfway through the song, when the audience started to drum softly on the table. Two rather tall, brawny young men sporting feather headdresses walked up behind Peadar. What the feck are they up to, Fionn thought. Are they going to pick him up and toss him out the door? Then he saw a couple more boys, dressed similarly, walk up behind the rest of them. Jayz, he had to act swiftly or maybe they'd be tossed into a barbecue pit.

He caught Peadar's eye at a lull in the melody, then switched into a fast-paced jig called "Tobin's Favorite." The drumming was replaced by clapping and soon people were up and dancing, arms linked like barrel monkeys as they spun around the dance floor.

"Keep it goin'," Fionn yelled. They morphed the tune into a fast-paced reel called "Toss the Feathers." The audience began to whoop. All the commotion stirred the Grand Drummer from his seat at the head table. He strutted up to the dance floor and stood atop a log that two of the brawny boys placed on the floor. He was wearing an "apron" with long fake feathers attached. When he pressed a switch on the waistband, the feathers started to drum the log. Everyone pounded their fists on the tables, keeping rhythm with the Grand Drummer. The ruckus was so loud, the musicians couldn't hear themselves.

The Grand Drummer looked around the lodge at the frenzied audience and smiled. Then he pressed the switch once more and his feathers stopped drumming the log instantly. The bartender caught Diarmuid's eye, and "slashed" his hand palm down across his throat.

"Stop," Diarmuid mouthed to Fionn as the brawny boys moved closer to them.

The band halted mid-tune as everyone watched the Grand Drummer remove his feather apron reverently and hand it to a brawny boy who folded it carefully into a gilded wooden box. He locked the box, gave the key to the Grand Drummer, then the brawny boys escorted him out of the lodge and drove him away in a black Escalade.

"Did we offend someone?" Peadar asked, looking around at the crowd emptying out of the lodge.

"Dunno, lad," Fionn said.

"What do we do now?" Aisling asked, sliding the accordion's straps off her shoulders. Diarmuid set down his guitar and walked over to the bar.

"Say, can ye tell me what's goin' on here, lad?"

A lodge member sipping a beer answered before the bartender could. "Once the Grand Drummer's done, the evening's over. You never can tell when he's supped his fill."

"So, we haven't offended anyone then?"

"No way, dude," the bartender said as he popped peanuts into his mouth. "Actually, looked like the old poobah got a kick outta you guys."

Brian walked over to speak with Fionn. Peadar and Aisling wondered if he was going to pay them for their performance.

"Thanks for lettin' us play here, Brian. It was a fun evening,"

Fionn said as he extended his hand.

"Listen here, Fionn," Brian replied, poking him in the chest, spit sliding out of the corner of his mouth. "You and your stupid band can find somewhere else to spend the night. How *dare* you interrupt Kelli's well-deserved applause like that! Do you know what this evening meant to her? She's been practicing that medley for months. You come over here showing off, thinking you're so Irish," he said wagging his finger at the others.

"That's because we *are* so Irish, ye *cabóg*," Diarmuid snickered.

"I don't want any lip from *you*, Mr. I-R-A!" Brian yelled, pointing at Diarmuid as if his fingers were a gun. "As far as I'm concerned, you and your IRA buddy Michael Flatley can go back on the boat that brought you over! To hell with you all!"

"Flatley? Ha-*ha*! What the? He was born in America, ye eejit!" Diarmuid yelled.

"But you don't deny he's in the IRA, now, do you!" Brian responded at equal volume. Diarmuid backed away laughing hysterically. Michael Flatley in the IRA? Ha-*hah*! Absofeckin' ridiculous!

His laughter infuriated Brian and he stormed out of the lodge as Aisling raised her hand to say, "Wait! What about our clothes?"

"Don't worry, dudes," the bartender said as he closed up the bar. "No prob, you can all crash at my place. I'd give you a lift, but after my latest DWI, they took my license away. It's not that far though, about a mile down the road. Easy walk. By the way, I'm Mick," he said, hand extended. They all waved their hands limply at him. No energy left for a proper shake.

Aisling looked worried. Diarmuid leaned over and gave her a hug.

"We'll be OK, girl."

"But our suitcases ... clothes ...."

"Aw, Brian's got a bad temper but after he blows up, he's usually cool the next day," Mick said. "He's way sensitive about his girls. Almost punched me out the time he caught me talking with Katie in the parking lot." Fionn nodded at Mick and gritted his teeth as he calculated what he thought Katie's age must be—he knew it was nowhere near the age of consent.

"So, are you dudes pumped for parade day tomorrow?"

"What's this parade day yer talkin' about?" Peadar asked as he set the pipes in their case.

"What parade? Aren't you dudes supposed to be Irish? St. Patty's, of course!"

"A St. Paddy's Day parade?" Diarmuid asked in a corrective tone.

"Yeah, d'oh! St. Patty's." Mick shook his head. Man these Irish dudes are slow on the uptake.

"But it's just March 10. Why so early?" Peadar asked.

"That way we get some major pipe bands in from out of town."

"Is yer parade big?"

"Dude, it's ginormous!"

"Out here, in the country?"

"Well, we hold the Guinness Book of World Records for the biggest vat of Irish stew. It's made in Vern Watson's cow pasture in a silo cut in half and turned on its side. They also have an all-green breakfast: green eggs, green SPAM cutlets shaped like shamrocks, green English muffins." Diarmuid laughed out loud. "Then there's the unlimited tap. A tank car with a tap sits on the train tracks that cut through Vern's property. It's filled with green beer. Draws in all the college kids from around here. They trek through the wet field and get plastered with mud. After they throw back a few drafts, it gets pretty gnarly."

"Define gnarly," Diarmuid said as he picked up his guitar case and walked out the door with the rest.

"Dude, it's like *Girls Gone Wild* on crack!"

Aisling cringed. Fionn walked over and put his arm around her. "Don't worry, luv. I'll keep ye safe."

They followed Mick down the country road in a single file, minding the pickups whizzing past. Aisling started thinking about that growing list in her mind of things as fearful as death by coyotes. She wondered if the Ruffed Grousers might be shoved off the list by rough paraders.

Mick lived on the second floor of a duplex, above a gun and bait shop. They climbed the narrow stairs at the back of his building and waited on the small porch as he unlocked the door.

"Gotta warn you guys," Mick laughed, "it's a bit of a mess in here." As they entered a tiny kitchen an orange tabby cat rushed out to greet them, rubbing their legs as she purred.

"Pretty kitty. What's her name?" Aisling said, stooping to pet the cat.

"Bambi. I swear she's got eyes like a baby deer."

"Absolutely, Mick. Soulful eyes," she said as the cat rubbed its head into the palm of her hand.

Peadar looked at the pile of dirty dishes in the sink and cringed. Diarmuid saw the case of beer next to the fridge and smiled. Fionn was just grateful to be out of feckin' Paddy MacSeamus land.

"Let me give you a tour, dudes." Mick walked out of the kitchen into the living room. "This pulls out for two," he said, sweeping a pile of empty beer cans off the cushions and tossing some empty pork rind bags behind the couch. "That recliner pushes way back. Someone could sleep there, too," he said pointing at a chair covered in matted red velour. "There's also a camo sleeping bag that I use during deer season. Sorry there's dried deer blood and gristle on it, but it's on the outside so you don't have to worry. Someone can use it on the floor here." Peadar's mouth turned downward as he grimaced. "Of course, there's always room in my bed if someone gets a little cold."

Whoa there ruffed grousers and rough paraders, Aisling thought to herself, we have a new list leader.

"Sorry, lad. That's me duty, keeping her warm," Fionn said as he drew Aisling close to give the impression that they were a couple. Thank ye, oh thank ye, Fionn, Aisling thought as she hugged him back tightly. Diarmuid frowned and crossed his arms. Mick noticed his reaction and thought, whoa, looks like a love triangle.

"So, anyone want a brewskie?" Mick rubbed his hands together.

Peadar shook his head. "There's a recliner with me name on it. Good night all."

"I'm kinda tired, too," Aisling said.

"C'mon luv, lets make the bed then." Fionn said as he took the cushions off the couch and pulled it out into a sleeper. Mick brought out some fleece blankets that didn't quite cover the chair or couch, but they were better than nothing. He set the camouflage-print sleeping bag on the floor.

"How about you, dude?" Mick asked Diarmuid. "You look like you could use a brew or two."

"Or three or four," Diarmuid laughed as he sat down at the kitchen table opposite Mick. They flipped the beer pull tabs open, then clicked their cans.

"*Sláinte*," Diarmuid said.

"Huh?"

"Cheers!"

"OK, gotcha, dude. You guys speak English mostly like us, but some of those words you use I've never heard."

"That's because they're Irish, Mick."

"Like your own slang?"

"Like our own feckin' language!"

"Dude, that's so cool."

"Yeah, we know."

"So," Mick said looking around to see if the others were listening. "Tell me about bein' in the IRA. Have you blown up people, buildings?"

Diarmuid sat back in his chair and sized up the young man across from him. Should I be nice, or have a bit of sport, he wondered. No harm done as long as I'm pleasant to the lad, right?

"Of course. It's feckin' *brilliant* to see somethin' go KABOOM!" He held out his arms wide as he bulged his eyes.

Mick was nodding his head, as if he knew what Diarmuid was talking about.

"One time there was this poor aul cratur who got in the way—a fishmonger named Willie Joe. Boom! The car bomb explodes and doesn't his bleedin' eyeball fly off and hit me in the shoulder where I was hidin'."

"No way, dude. That's so twisted! Whaddya do with it?"

"Gave it a proper burial."

Mick pointed his beer can at Diarmuid. "I like you bro. You've got scruples,"

"Yer right there, boyo," Diarmuid winked.

"So, are you on Ireland's Most Wanted List?"

"Nah, I'm small potatoes. The one they're really after is in the other room."

"The tall dude?"

"Fionn? Nah!"

"Ashley?"

Diarmuid laughed as he shook his head.

"*No way,* man, that little guy? Really? But he seems so, I don't know, girly."

"That's how he cons his victims. Cold-blooded murderer, he is. I've seen him kill troops, pregnant women, even puppies."

"Puppies! Dude, that's just *wrong*." Mick sat back in his chair, eyes wide, pondering how he'd misjudged the little man asleep in the recliner. "Dude, can I beer you another?"

"Yeah, dude," Diarmuid said, laughing at his own use of Yank lingo. "Beer me two. Deadly thirst upon me."

"Wow, I heard you guys were partiers."

"Got any crisps here?"

"Huh?"

"Crisps, ye know, potato crisps? Taytos?"

"Dude, I'm like totally losing you. What's that, breakfast cereal or something?"

"Hah! No, ye know, thin slices of potatoes, fried and salted."

"Oh, CHIPS. Yeah, hold on." Mick pulled a bag out of the cupboard and ripped it open. "So, dude, does bein' in the IRA help you score with hot chicks?"

"Oh, does it! Fightin' them away every night, then they fight with each other over yez, awful tough."

"Man, I love watchin' chicks fight," Mick said as he let out an exaggerated cat purr.

"Who doesn't," Diarmuid grinned. "Mick, ye seem like a trustworthy lad. Mind if I tell ye an IRA secret?"

"Really? You'd trust me with that? Dude! That's *awesome!*"

"OK, but you must promise not to tell anyone. We have ways of findin' out, ye know, very well connected here in the States."

"Cross my heart with my pinky swear."

"This is secret IRA code for identifying that you agree with our cause and ye hate the bloody English."

"Yeah the fookers!"

"Good lad there. I can feckin' tell already that yer one of us. So here's the code, ready?"

Mick nodded, heart pounding at the gravity of the moment.

"When we greet each other this time of year, we say 'Happy St. Paddy's Day.'"

"That's it? Happy St. Patty's Day?"

"No, listen carefully. Not T, it's D. Ye see, the word for Patrick in our language is *Pádraig*. So if ye say Patty with a d, *Paddy*, it shows ye believe in the Irish language and our nation reunited."

Mick sat back in the chair, swigged his beer then extended his hand to Diarmuid.

"Happy St. Paddy's Day, bro," he said.

"Happy St. Paddy's Day, dude," Diarmuid said with as serious an expression as he could muster. They clicked beer cans again. Bambi came into the room and jumped onto Mick's lap. As he petted her, he thought, boy, his life couldn't get much better. Here he was, part of the IRA brotherhood now. He wished he could repay his new friend Diarmuid some way.

Mick, being a bartender at the lodge since he was 16, had the gift as they say. That is, he possessed a gift for listening to people blather on about their troubles. The Grand Drummer had even confided to him once that he had a horrible fear of wood splinters. He was petrified that during one of his displays at a lodge gathering, a feather might fling a pointy one up from the log into his nether zone.

Mick already picked up the vibe that Diarmuid was in love with that Ashley. Perhaps if he could get him drunk, Diarmuid would spill his guts to him and Mick could help him deal with the unrequited relationship.

"Ever do a shooter, bro?"

"Yer asking that of an IRA man?"

"I know, like d'oh!" Mick snorted. "I mean a beer shooter. You use a can opener to poke a hole in the bottom of the can, see.

Shake the can real hard, then pop the top and let the beer spray into your mouth all at once. It's a rush, man. Way better than doobage."

"Set me up then, Mick."

He got the can ready, had Diarmuid cover the bottom hole and shake the can wildly. "Ready, dude?"

Within a half hour, Diarmuid had professed his undying love for Aisling to Mick. The story went that they had met last year because she was dating his friend Eamon, her classmate at the university in Galway. Diarmuid felt something for her instantly and wanted to spend more time with her but Eamon was always there. Then one day he ran into her as she busked on Shop Street. She was playing "My Darling Asleep" on her accordion. "Och, her playin' was savage, just brilliant," Diarmuid said. They'd had a lovely chat up for more than an hour about music, but that was all.

A month ago he went with Eamon to catch the session at The Vestibule on a Tuesday night. His heart nearly stopped when he saw her there. Aisling had played in Fionn's first incarnation of Slí na Fírinne. That's why she was jamming with him, Peadar (who was in town with a Comhaltas group) and the other trad musicians.

He remembered how she looked so at ease with the other musicians that night. Diarmuid thought it was probably because she came from a trad music dynasty. Her father—a well-known fiddler—led the popular Ballinfoyle Céilí Band and her mother, also a button accordion player, had a weekly trad music show on Raidío na Gaeltachta. Eamon said Aisling had been playin' the button accordion since she was four. By the age of 16, she'd won the All-Ireland title at the fleadh for the 15-18 group.

It was such a different upbringing than Diarmuid's. His Da

took off one day for a job prospect abroad in Barcelona and never returned, leaving the family scrambling for income. His Ma took in laundry and worked summers at Salthill's amusement park for many years. When she got sick, he dropped out of school and did odd jobs in the seaside casinos and restaurants to help support the family. Some of his mates started a Waterboys tribute band and they played a few gigs on The Prom (as Salthill's seaside promenade is called). Ever since he'd been in a series of bands—some trad, some rock. He moved out of the family home when his recuperated mother turned it into a bed and breakfast for summer tourists. It didn't take him long to get on his feet and put his own roof over his head. Diarmuid found a job driving a delivery truck for a seafood distributor during the day. At night he roved the trad sessions around Galway.

Thank God Diarmuid had brought along his guitar to that Tuesday night session. He joined in on some tunes and Fionn told Diarmuid he liked his playing. He asked if Diarmuid would be interested in joining his new band. Of course he said yes. Then when Fionn mentioned his plan for a tour in the States, Diarmuid was over the moon. Here was a rare opportunity to get to know a girl out of his league better. He'd have alone time with lovely Aisling here in America, they'd share some great experiences and hopefully by the time they'd get back to Galway, she'd have to break the bad news to Eamon. But then Fionn wrecked the car and things weren't going exactly as he'd planned.

"Dude, have you told her how you feel about her?"

"Why the feck would I do that? That'd be just settin' me up fer disaster."

"Well, show her by your actions that you dig her."

"I wish Fionn hadn't lied to ye about them being together," Diarmuid said, head resting on the table. It felt oddly heavy for some reason.

"Whoa, man, didn't think about it. That dude lied to me," he swigged more beer and frowned. "Hey, you're IRA. You should pop him dude, for messin' with your lady. I can get you a gun. From downstairs. I sneak into the gun shop all the time to get ammunition for deer season."

"No. That wouldn't solve the problem. She'd mourn his death, hate me forever." Diarmuid sighed and rested his head on his folded hands.

Mick nodded his head then took another swig of his beer.

"OK then, listen. Why don't you go in there now, while he's asleep, kneel down next to the couch and profess your love to her?"

Diarmuid waved his arm and shook his head. "Nah, she'd think I was bleedin' demented or a sicko, creepin' up to her like that while she was sleepin'."

"Hmm, yeah, probably right dude."

After an hour more of drinking shooters, Diarmuid staggered to his feet.

"Mick, me boyo, I'm gonna do it. Gonna let Aisling know me true feelings. Who gives a feck about Eamon? Eamon can feckin' *póg mo thóin*!"

"Yeah, feckin' Eamon! One thing though, dude. I think her name is *Ashley*. Better get it right." Diarmuid threw his head back laughing then pointed his hand at Mick as if it was a gun.

"Happy St. Paddy's Day, boyo."

"Happy feckin' St. Paddy's Day, bro!"

Diarmuid staggered over to the couch where Aisling slept.

"*Jaysus*! She's so feckin' gorgeous! *Deadly* gorgeous!"

Mick laughed. "Shhhh! Don't want to wake the others," Diarmuid said, trying to locate his mouth so he could put his finger in front of it to signal silence. He went to pat Aisling's head, missed, lost his footing and fell on top of her. Fionn jumped up with a start. They could hear Aisling's muffled voice under Diarmuid's drunk-heavy body.

"Diarmuid, yer bleedin' wrecked. Get off the girl!"

Diarmuid somehow staggered to his feet but then fell onto the carpet and passed out.

"I thought the coyotes had come to get me," Aisling said, terrified as she grabbed Fionn's shirt. "What just happened?"

"Well, I'm here to protect ye, but I didn't expect it would be from that beast," Fionn said looking at Diarmuid splayed on the floor. Mick also seemed to be having difficulty staying vertical.

"Like later, dudes. Gotta go hurl." He stumbled off toward the bathroom just in time. The noise of his retching awakened Peadar.

"*Jaysus*, what the feck's goin' on here? Diarmuid's dead, someone's dyin' in the jacks and yez...." He stared at Aisling hugging Fionn. "Holy mother of God, what a bloody nightmare. I shoulda stayed home in Mayo. Me Da was right when he said yez were worse than knackers and I'd taint me clean Comhaltas image by hanging out with the likes of yez."

Aisling noticed how nice it felt to have Fionn's strong arms around her. It was funny. She'd hardly thought about her boyfriend

Eamon at all on this trip. Wonder if he was thinking about her, back in Galway?

Peadar pulled the fleece blanket around his neck, exposing his holey socks to the cold air in Mick's apartment. He started thinking about his mother's apple cake, and how he'd love a slice of it with a nice cuppa Barry's.

Diarmuid thrashed and tossed through tortured sleep, ducking flying eyeballs. Mick, who chose to sleep next to the toilet, dreamed he was saying "Happy St. Paddy's Day" to everyone in the parade, then laughed to himself because they didn't know what he was *really* saying. Fionn was wide awake, not a thought crossing his mind, just a general sense of ominous times ahead. Aisling had fallen asleep and was snoring lightly. Fionn wondered, should he move her gently back to her side of the bed or let her sleep in his arms? He had to admit, it did feel good to hold her close. All the time he was with Renny, they'd never shared a tender moment like this. Another red flag he'd missed. Jaysus, he thought, am I feckin' color blind?

FÁINNE #3

Tubas? Bloody tubas! Diarmuid winced as he raised one eyebrow, then shrugged his whole body. A brass band blared "It's A Great Day For The Irish" from the bed of a pickup truck passing Mick's house. The tinny music warbled down the road as the rest of the band woke up whining.

"Jayz, what time is it?" Peadar asked.

"Jayz, what day is it?" Diarmuid said as he sat up, felt the jackhammers drilling in his head and plopped back on the floor.

"Hey, boyo, ye didn't sleep in yer bloody sleeping bag." Fionn laughed as he stood up and stretched his arms toward the ceiling then bent them behind his back.

"He was too busy trying to attack me," Aisling teased. "Diarmuid, ye old shape shifter. Thought yez was a coyote last night, eh? That's what the drink'll do to yez."

"I was only after a few beers."

"C'mon, now. How much did yez two really have?" Peadar said, as he stood over his helpless looking bandmate.

"Not much, just a couple of shooters. Maybe four."

"What's a shooter, Diarmuid?"

He winced at the daylight permeating the room. "It's a way to drink an entire beer all at once."

"Och! Yer lucky to be alive, ye gobshite." Peadar shook his

head as he folded the fleece blanket into a tidy square.

"Is our host asleep still?" Fionn asked as he walked toward the bathroom to use it. He caught a whiff of the foulness slithering out the slightly ajar door. "*Jayz*! Shite and onions!"

"Is he in there? Is he alive?" Aisling asked.

"Well... don't think he's gonna be bartendin' today. Let's get out of here while we still can."

They grabbed their instruments, tiptoed down the back stairs and walked out front to the road.

"Which way now, fearless leader?" Aisling asked, grinning at Fionn.

"Let's head toward the sun. Turn left."

It was an unseasonably warm March morning, already into the high 40s. Diarmuid squinted toward the sky and felt his temples throbbing. He rubbed his eyes, picked up the guitar case and trailed behind the others. They could hear the wail of bagpipes in the distance. Oh bloody hell, Diarmuid thought, that's all I need now. Soon they passed cars and trucks parked on both shoulders of the road, forcing them to walk on the grass to keep out of traffic safely.

"What's that smell? It's like burning dog meat," Peadar said.

"Not even goin' to ask ye," Aisling said, voice drowned out by the approaching snare drums.

A bouquet of green clover-shaped balloons tethered to a weather vane danced over a barn up ahead. The band members saw half of a silo lying on a makeshift cinder block grill nearby. A pair of brawny boys from the Ruffed Grouse Lodge's hooley stirred a liver brown mixture cooking there—this year's attempt at breaking the Guinness World Record for Largest Irish Stew.

"Och that smells disgustin'," Diarmuid said, holding his stomach.

"That must be the green beer train!" Peadar pointed toward a black container car on the tracks at the bottom of the cow pasture.

"Good thing we're comin' through here now," Fionn said, "or else we'd be seein' a lot more of what yer man Mick was spewin' last night."

"Lovely, thanks for that imagery. A whole different interpretation of four green fields." Aisling tried to think of happier things, such as fluttering butterflies or kittens knitting their paws into balls of string. Nope. Didn't work.

"I wonder what last night would have been like if we'd stayed with the Murphys?" Diarmuid asked.

"Them girls would have been practicin' like fiends for today. Kelli would be there with her metronome, waggin' her finger at us that we were playin' too slow." Peadar mimed the mother videotaping with one hand, keeping time with the other.

"Aisling, I mean *Ashley*, would have been refereeing the upstairs cat fights," Fionn laughed.

"Well, I don't think her sleeping arrangements last night were much better." Diarmuid winced as he rubbed his aching forehead.

"I have no complaints." Aisling grinned. Diarmuid frowned. Why the feck did he open up to that eejit Mick about his feelings for her? And after he fell on her last night, Aisling probably thought he was a pervy sicko, too. His temples throbbed as pipe band snare drums rat-a-tat-tatted around him.

"Don't yez think we ought to go the other way?" Peadar

asked. "Looks like there's no way around this parade." He was right. A wave of green-clad humanity rolled toward them. The crest of the crowd was so large, it had already splashed onto the pasture.

"Maybe if we just stand still they'll go around us, and when they've passed, we can continue on our way?" Diarmuid rested his guitar case upright on the road and leaned on it. Fionn looked back at where they'd come from, then turned to view the road ahead.

"Jaysus!" Fionn said. "This crowd's about to make a Slí na Fírinne sandwich. Look at what's chasing us!"

A big ladder truck from the Homer Fire Department cruised up behind them. It stopped across from the giant "stew pot" and started blaring its siren. Diarmuid doubled over, covering his ears. Aisling went over and put her arm around him.

"Ye all right there, luv?"

He shook his head. She looked at a hill on the other side of the road. "Ye know, if we climbed over there, we could hide from all this insanity until it passes."

"Good idea there, lass," Diarmuid said. "Let's go."

The hill was muddy from all the recent snow melt. They struggled to climb up it without losing their footing. Peadar especially had difficulty. His ankle wobbled over the uneven terrain. Near the top of the hill was a flat boulder with room for all of them to sit down. They rested there and watched the parade passing by below.

There were pipe bands, step dancers (the McCool School was first in line), more fire trucks, county road plows, sheriff's deputies tossing green lollipops, councilmen throwing hard green taffy bits, Scout troops, women riding Appaloosa horses, 4H Club teens walking a pair of scruffy wolfhounds and a group of middle-aged women wearing shamrock sweatshirts and sunglasses as they banged pots with spoons to a recording of Paddy MacSeamus singing "The Irish Washerwoman."

"Feck all. He's everywhere! Why can't I get away from his shite?" Fionn yelled, standing up and looking ready to lob a rock at the speakers on the truck in front of the women.

"*Suigh síos!*" Peadar said, tugging at Fionn's shirt. "Give it a rest, lad. Nuttin' ye can do about it."

"With all the beautiful Irish music in the world, it's just ...."

"We hear ye, Fionn. Take yer ease. We can still have a good laugh watchin' this spectacle."

Fionn plopped down between Aisling and Diarmuid. There Fionn goes, closing in on me territory, Diarmuid thought. He had to make a move. Diarmuid leaned back and put his arm around Aisling, pointing at the old woman wearing giant leprechaun ears, curled gold slippers and a wig of thick orange yarn.

"That one's always after me Lucky Charms," Diarmuid said. Aisling laughed.

"Do ye suppose I'll look like that when I'm that age?" she asked him, smiling.

"Ye'll look more like that," Fionn said, pointing at the Maid of Tara, a pretty young girl in medieval dress wearing a tiara and cloak with embroidered shamrocks. Aisling patted his knee. "Good answer, Fionn."

Behind the Maid of Tara, a high school band played the "Notre Dame Victory March." A random old man with a blue and gold sweatshirt and Kelly green tam-o-shanter wandered down the road next to them thrusting a shillelagh into the air like he was their drum major. Next came a line of tractors, manure spreaders and combines blaring their horns, making Diarmuid wince. Aisling helped him cover his ears, and Diarmuid prayed silently for more. By the time the last float passed, the pasture on the other side of the road was completely filled with people.

Scratchy music blasted out of the loudspeakers hung from the telephone poles lining Vern Warner's property. Some local folk singers performing on the barn stage strummed banjos while singing "Charlie On The MTA." When they got to the chorus, a large group of college students shouted "Oi! Oi! Oi!" then broke into a manic jig, dancing with arms akimbo.

"*Jaysus*, will yez look at them. It's not even noon and they're feckin' langers!" Diarmuid laughed.

"Don't ye think they're havin' more fun than us though?" Aisling sat with arms folded over her crossed legs that kept time with the music.

"Go on then, girl," Diarmuid said as he jumped up, took her hand and started aping the crowd's MTA jig, pausing every once in a while to throw back his head and yell, "Oi! Oi! Oi!" Aisling was laughing so hard she could barely dance. Soon Peadar sprung from the boulder, scratched his head like a chimpanzee and linked his arm with Aisling as he limped around the rock. Fionn shook his head at his bandmates. They did look like they were havin' fun. What was the harm?

"All right, ye eejits. Move over." Fionn jumped into the fray and started spinning around and shouting "Oi! Oi! Oi!" with the others. His arm was linked with Aisling's when the song ended and the folk group started playing an old-time waltz. He grabbed Aisling's hand, gave her a quick twirl then waltzed around with her. Peadar stopped and smiled. Diarmuid grabbed his forehead as his headache returned.

Aisling liked the feel of her hand in Fionn's. She had no idea he was such a good dancer. As the tune drew to a close, he spun her around a few times more then dipped her for the big finish. It left her breathless. It left him with a flashback of Renny. He released Aisling like her touch had burned him and sat back on the boulder to brood.

Of course Diarmuid noticed she was blushing as she sat down next to him on the boulder. That didn't happen when he took her for a spin. Och, he felt like death warmed over again. A shift of the wind carried smells of the dreadful stew below. Diarmuid's stomach fluttered. Please God, he thought, don't let me get sick in front of her. He got up and wandered away to get some fresh air.

The others didn't notice he'd left. They were too distracted by the weird mob below. "Look at that decadence," Peadar hissed. "Them people below look like somethin' out of a Hieronymus Bosch painting. What does any of this have to do with St. Patrick?"

Back down the road a few miles, Mick woke up from a horrid sleep at his apartment, took a shower and cleaned up the bathroom mess. He was sorry to see that his new IRA buddy had left. They must have gone to the parade already, he thought. Then he noticed their instruments were gone, too. They'd split, without so much as a thank you. That's the way those IRA-ers roll, he guessed.

Mick donned a green plastic bowler hat, Guinness T-shirt

and shamrock glasses as he jogged down the steps and headed for the festivities. By then the traffic had backed up all the way to the front of his home. Most of the people wandering about were out-of-town college students. Many of them were halfway on the road to "Blottoville" by the time Mick arrived at Vern's farm.

As he was eating a bowl of the stew, he noticed a cluster of young men who had accents like that Diarmuid fella. Bet they're IRA, he thought. He finished the stew, threw away his garbage and approached the men.

"Happy St. *Paddy's* Day," he said to them and winked.

"What the feck's *yer* problem?" one asked, stepping back from him.

"You know, *Paddy*. Not *Patty*." Mick stood there nodding his head.

"Bugger off, ye wanker!" The young men laughed and walked down the field toward the railroad car field with green beer.

Mick smiled. Scared them off 'cause they knew I'm part of the IRA brethren, he thought. Man. You're such a badass, Mick, he laughed to himself.

"Wait a minute. Hey Mr. Shamrock Glasses!" the young men called out to him. Mick walked down to where they were standing.

"Wassup, o'peeps?"

The Irishman leaned toward Mick and whispered, "Not sure how ye knew we're in the fookin' IRA, but listen Yank, we were just wonderin' where ye could buy some cheap ammo around here?"

"Oh yeah, you're talkin' to the right guy," Mick said nodding his head as the others huddled around him.

Diarmuid was having a terrible time settling his stomach

down. He'd walk a bit, then double over ready to vomit. The nausea wave passed, he stood up and grasped the branch of a sumac bush to regain his balance. Wait a minute, was he hearing things, or was that harp music in the distance? He tried to concentrate on the sound but it was difficult to separate it from the parade day din in the background. That's got to be a harp, but where was it coming from, he wondered. Another wave of nausea hit him, then he began to think, am I dying? Have I already died and I just have to follow the harp music? Diarmuid walked through a small thicket of oak trees to where he saw a woman playing an O'Carolan tune on a Celtic harp. She was seated in the center of a flagstone labyrinth behind an old farmhouse. Her ethereal music stunned him—it was such a contrast to the cartoonish crap playing down the hill. Each note she plucked compelled Diarmuid to draw closer to her.

The woman had silky fawn-brown hair and wore a handwoven smock in saturated hues of teal and hunter green. She smiled as she played, and Diarmuid was drawn to the dimples on her rose-colored cheeks. *This* was a vision! But wait—could this be some sort of sorcery, a cruel mirage? He edged closer and his foot crunched rotted acorns on the grass. The woman looked up, startled to see him there. She grabbed the harp and raced toward the farmhouse door.

"Wait, don't run away. I won't hurt ye. I'm an Irish musician, too. Visiting here from Galway. Our band's on tour. It's just such a pleasure to hear some *real* Irish music."

The woman eyed him carefully as she tried to figure out if he was worth her trust.

"Where in Galway?" she asked in a soft but measured tone.

"Salthill."

"What's your surname?"

"Kinsella. I'm Diarmuid Kinsella."

She tilted her head and eyed him up and down. "'The Pipe On The Hob.' Is it a reel or a hornpipe?"

"Neither. It's a jig."

She smiled and allowed Diarmuid to approach her. From a distance he noted her eyes were bright as crystal blue sapphires caught in sunlight.

"Why are ye playin' yer harp outside?"

"Just wanted to muffle the noise of the rabble-rousers over on Vern's property. Can't stand that schlock *they* call Irish music. I'm Danu by the way."

Hmm, named for an Irish goddess, he thought. Perfect. She looked like one all right. He took her hand as she extended it. "Lovely to meet ye. Listen, would ye mind if I brought the rest of me band over here to meet ye?"

"How many are you?"

"Just four."

"Of course, they're welcome in this place. Would you care for some tea?"

"Och, that'd be grand. Give me a few and I'll be back with the rest."

Diarmuid's nausea vanished and he ran as fast as he could to tell the others the good news, that for the first time since the accident, he'd met someone "normal," someone who understood Irish music. He was breathless by the time he reached the boulder.

"Really? A harpist playin' O'Carolan here? In this

godforsaken place?" Fionn's eyes grew wider with each nod of Diarmuid's head. "Lead the way, lad. Let's get the feck out of here!"

They knocked on Danu's door and dogs on the other side responded with fierce barking.

"Hope they're not relatives of Virgil's beasts," Peadar muttered.

Danu opened the door and beckoned them inside. It was a lovely farmhouse, decorated simply, and her two border collies had barks much more ferocious than their temperaments.

"Come and sit while I heat some water for the tea. Are you hungry? I made some soup for my lunch and there's plenty to go around."

"That'd be grand," Fionn said, smiling at her as he pulled out a Shaker chair from the table to sit down. He rested his elbows on the table, clasped his hands together and watched with rapt attention as Danu filled the teapot at the sink, set it on the stove, then lifted the lid on the soup pot and gave it a stir. Aisling noticed that the men smiled very easily at this woman and were completely fascinated with her every movement. She wasn't what you'd call beautiful, Aisling thought. Danu had a thin face, square jaw and sinewy arms, yet she was wide of hip. She reminded Aisling of the hippies hawking fair trade clothing in the Galway Market on Church Lane.

"Is that brown bread?" Diarmuid said as Danu carried a basket to the table with the teapot.

"Yes, I made it a little while ago."

"Ye sure know the way to an Irishman's heart," Peadar said, looking at her like she was a slice of his mother's apple cake.

"I'd second that," Fionn said as he bit into the still warm bread that he slathered with fresh, farm-made butter.

Aisling sat there silently, noting the curious reactions of the men.

"I hope you all like corned beef. This is my take on it, actually more of a stew than soup. It's made with free range beef and organic vegetables."

Ugh. Not corned beef again, Aisling thought. Don't Americans eat anything else?

"Och, I *love* it," Diarmuid said. Huh? Aisling thought Diarmuid was always the first to criticize the fatty hunks of salt-cured meat.

"Nothin' better," Peadar added.

"I hope there's enough for seconds," Fionn said with the robotic enthusiasm of a cult member.

Their odd behavior stunned Aisling. She knew they all hated corned beef and cabbage. Why the sudden turnabout? That Danu had an air about her that they were responding to eagerly. Did she bathe herself in pheromones? That might explain why the lads were simply gawking at her. Look at them, Aisling thought, all lined up like dogs with their tongues panting out at Danu. What did she have that was turning them on so?

The conversation at lunch was all about Danu and the session she ran on Sunday afternoons at an old Quaker meeting house down the road. Aisling played with a soup spoon as Danu droned on.

"Would you all like to could come to it?" Danu asked. "We get a good turnout usually. I'm sure the regulars would love the opportunity to play with some musicians from Ireland."

Fionn looked at the others. "I'm sure in. Sounds like fun. How about the rest of yez?" Diarmuid nodded as he beamed at Danu. Same with Peadar. Aisling sat there with no expression.

"How about you?" Danu asked Aisling, her piercing blue eyes probing her reaction.

"Well, we were heading out of town before we met ye. We're booked for some gigs this week and really should be on our way."

"But where will we stay tonight?" Peadar protested. "We have nowhere to go."

"Is that true?" Danu asked.

"Yes, luv. The lad we were stayin' with last night is not feelin' well and there really wasn't enough room for us there." Peadar shrugged his shoulders, frowned as sadly as he could while jutting out his lower lip, hoping for an invite.

"Well, there's plenty of room in my home. I'd be honored if you'd stay the night."

"Och, the honor is all *ours*, Danu," Diarmuid said, nearly drooling on her.

Jaysus, what disgustin' fools, Aisling thought. All of 'em. Stumbling over each other, just to chat up this homely earth mother.

"Would anyone like dessert?" Danu smiled as she cleared the table. The men nodded eagerly. "And what about *you*, Aisling?" She grunted a response that sounded affirmative.

"Don't go anywhere. I'll be right back."

The men's eyes were riveted to Danu as she stepped up out of the dining room into the kitchen. Aisling was ticked at their rudeness. Had they forgotten another girl was in the room?

"Fionn, have ye tried yer mobile again?" Aisling asked, breaking his concentration on Danu's curvy hips.

"Ye know, I forgot all about it." He pulled out the phone from his jacket pocket. "Uh-oh," he said.

"No bars?" Peadar frowned.

"Worse. The battery's dead. Must have left it on when I checked it last night. The charger's in me suitcase, now being held captive by the Murphys."

Aisling's face went pale. Oh no, would they never get home now?

"Maybe Danu has a mobile charger ye could use," Aisling said brightly.

"Oh, she's got a charger all right," Diarmuid smirked. The men all snickered.

"Yer nuthin' but pigs. Yez know that, right? Everyone of yez," Aisling said as she folded her arms and pouted.

"C'mon girl, we're just makin' sport," Fionn said. She looked away from him.

"Aren't ye even going to see if she has a land line we could use?"

"Ye know," Fionn said earnestly, "I never thought of that. Brilliant idea."

"It's not feckin' brilliant, it's feckin' *obvious*," Aisling snapped back at him. Fionn had little reaction to her terse words. In no time he was staring with the other lads at Danu preparing something in the kitchen.

She returned to the dining room with a tray holding a fancy-looking dessert and plates.

"I hope you all like sticky toffee pudding. It's an old family recipe."

"Like?" Peadar said, visibly salivating. "It's only me favorite dessert in the whole world, after me Ma's apple cake of course. She makes it only for special occasions."

"This is spooky," Diarmuid said with a serious face. "I was just thinking a second ago how I'd love a piece of sticky toffee pudding right now."

"Really? That's wonderful," Danu said as she cut the first slice for him.

"It's like ye can read me bleedin' mind or somethin'. Quick, what am I thinking now?"

Danu bent over and gave Diarmuid a kiss on his cheek.

"Jaysus! That's very, *very* close," he said winking at Aisling. She frowned as he looked back at their hostess.

"How about you, Fionn? Do you like sticky toffee pudding?"

He sat speechless, motionless, and as Aisling noted, breathless. It was as if Danu's looks had cryogenically frozen him.

"That's OK, you don't have to answer," she said as she slid a plate with a fork toward him. "Here you go."

He grinned at her and began eating his dessert slowly, never taking his eyes off her.

"Aisling, how big a slice would you like?" Danu said in a voice oozing with sweetness. Aisling scrunched her nose up.

"No thanks. On second thought I've got no room for it. Still full from the corned beef."

"Are you sure?"

"*Positive!*" As soon as the word passed over her lips, Aisling realized her tone might have sounded a bit harsh. "Oh, but it certainly does look delicious. By the way, Danu, do ye have a phone Fionn could borrow to call his cousin Des in Boston? We've got to get in touch with him. That's the only way we can contact the colleges on our tour to let them know about our car troubles. They need to know that we might not be showing up for some of our gigs."

"Phone? Silly Aisling. There's no need for a phone in this town. Everyone knows everyone else's business and we all help each other out."

"Ye don't have a phone? Are ye kiddin'? What do ye do if ye have an emergency or have to contact someone outside of the area?"

"I never have to. You see, Aisling, everything I want and need is already here, right before my eyes." She smiled at the three men and Aisling felt the hairs on the back of her neck stand up. "Would anyone mind if I got out my harp to practice? They say music aids digestion."

The men shook their heads 'no' in unison. Peadar noticed her harp was on a stand in the living room and stood up. "Here, let me get it for ye." As he walked across the room, the pain from his swollen ankle affected his gait.

"Peadar, are you limping?" Danu asked.

"Just a bit, it's nothin'. Banjaxed me ankle a couple of nights ago."

"Oh, lie down on that couch then and I can give you a crystal treatment."

Aisling snorted. Diarmuid and Fionn looked a bit jealous. Peadar lay down and looked up eagerly at Danu when she returned with a velvet pouch filled with crystals of different colors.

"What the feck, is she some sort of *cailleach*?" Aisling muttered to Fionn. He acted as if he didn't hear her at all. In fact, Aisling was beginning to notice the men were acting like zombies, that is, without all the oozing blood and dripping flesh. They had the zombie stare mastered all right, and it was creeping her out.

The thought occurred to Aisling that maybe Danu had put a potion in the dessert or cast a spell upon it. She was glad she hadn't eaten any. But was she really safe?

"Jaysus, yer a miracle worker, Danu!" Peadar stood up and walked around the room normally. "Me ankle feels brand new!"

"Ye know," Diarmuid interjected. "I have this terrible headache from last night. Do ye suppose yer rocks could help me too?" Danu waved him over to the couch and chanted an incantation in some quasi-Celtic tongue as she pressed crystals on his temples. He closed his eyes and appeared to be experiencing complete nirvana at her touch. When she stopped, he rubbed his hands where the crystals had been laid upon him and looked surprised.

"Ye know, I never believed all that New Age shite," Diarmuid said, "but ye've just made a convert out of me. It's like I never drank a drop last night. I'm a new man, strangely invigorated at the moment."

"How about you, Fionn?" Danu asked. "Anything, at all, that I can do for you?" For a brief moment he thought Danu's hair darkened and her face transformed into Renny's. Fionn's pulse quickened and he started biting the fingernail of his right thumb.

"Everything all right there, Fionn?" Aisling asked. She put her hand on his brow and noted that he felt feverish. Maybe he'd caught a cold from sitting on that boulder all day in the damp air.

"I have a special tea to break a fever," Danu said. In no time, the teakettle was whistling in the kitchen. The two border collies raced into the dining room as if on cue from the kettle and stopped on either side of Aisling. The black and white one started rubbing his head against her leg.

"That means he wants you to pet him," Danu said as she handed Fionn a cup of tea.

The red and white dog brought over a squeaky toy to Aisling.

"Throw it across the room for him. He loves to play fetch." Aisling tossed the fuzzy bone toward the back door and the red dog galloped after it, grabbed it in its teeth, shook it like a cocktail shaker then scampered back to her.

"Again?" Aisling laughed as she tossed it in the other direction. The black dog rubbed her leg again. She bent down to pet him and stroke his ears, but was interrupted when the red dog returned with the toy, biting it so it squeaked at her. She tugged the toy out of his mouth and tossed it away without looking as she gave the black dog a good chuck under his chin. The red dog was back, dropped the toy at her feet then stood there panting loudly, tail wagging furiously.

By the time the dogs finally tired out, Aisling looked up and noticed the three men and Danu were all gone. Where were they? She glanced around the kitchen and living room, then walked back outside onto the patio, but they were nowhere in sight.

"What the...?" She returned inside, checked all around her, but saw nothing but an empty living room and kitchen. Suddenly, a fatigue overcame Aisling that was so heavy she felt it literally push her down onto the couch. She propped a pillow behind her head, lifted her feet up and within seconds was sound asleep.

FÁINNE #4

Sunlight pierced star-shaped crystals hanging from the living room windows, splitting into tiny rainbows that danced across Aisling's face, nudging her gently awake. She rolled over on the couch and saw Danu and the men sipping tea at the dining room table.

"Hello again." Danu's cheerful greeting startled her. Aisling rubbed her eyes and looked around. The dogs were snoring by the back door. Something about the direction of light in the room seemed odd.

Aisling yawned as she strolled over to the table and plopped hard into a chair.

"Where've ye been?" she said as she poured a cup of tea.

"Huh?" Diarmuid said, giving her a look as if she was making no sense.

"Ye know, after dessert. I was playing with the dogs, looked up and suddenly yez were gone."

"Gone?" Peadar laughed heartily. "Ye were the one who was gone, luv. All of a sudden ye got up from the dinner table, lay down on the couch and fell asleep. It was odd, like ye were in a trance or something."

"How long was I asleep?"

"Give ye a clue, luv," Peadar said, patting her arm. "We're

ate'n breakfast now."

"Breakfast!" Aisling's eyes widened.

"I never saw ye playin' with them dogs," Fionn said.

"C'mon, stop coddin'me. The red dog was playin' fetch with his shaggy bone there. The black one was rubbin' me leg."

"Please luv, we don't need to hear the graphic details of yer kinky dreams." Diarmuid laughed.

"Are you in your moon time, Aisling?" Danu asked. "That might explain your sense of displacement. Here, have some corned beef quiche. The iron in it will be good for your troubles."

Aisling was confused. Had she dreamed all that she witnessed last night, with the lads acting all lovesick for Danu? Or was that woman really a witch and she'd cast a spell or something over the others? She nodded yes to Danu and began eating a slice of quiche. It wasn't lost on her, at that moment, that since they'd gotten lost in the backwoods of upstate New York, every meal they'd eaten included corned beef.

Peadar got up to use the bathroom and Aisling noticed he still had a limp. She looked at Diarmuid and he was rubbing his forehead.

"This bleedin' headache, will it ever leave?"

"What time is it?" Aisling asked as she poked at the quiche with her fork.

"I'd guess 10:45," Danu said. She sipped her tea while Aisling glanced around the room for a clock. "You won't find any timekeeper here. I depend on my senses to tell me what time of day it is. It worked good enough for the ancients."

Aisling smirked. She *is* a witch. "What would ye do if ye

lived by a volcano and it erupted, blacking out the sunlight? Would ye still be able to tell the time of day?" she asked coyly.

Danu handed the men a basket filled with cranberry scones fresh from the oven, then squinted at Aisling.

"Dear, we don't have volcanos in upstate New York. Your question is irrelevant."

"Can ye tell us where the nearest Catholic church is?" Peadar asked when he returned. "I'd like to catch Sunday Mass if we could."

Danu stood up from the table suddenly and disappeared into the kitchen without saying a word. Aisling leaned toward Peadar.

"I think she's a witch or a druid or somethin'. She put a spell on either me, ye lads or all of us last night. We've gotta get away from her, soon!"

Peadar sat back in his chair, his shoulders slumped and he pouted. "But, she doesn't look druish."

"I bet I can prove it. Give me a chance," Aisling whispered as Danu returned with her harp.

"Would you like to go over some of the tunes we play at our Sunday session, just to make sure that you're familiar with them?"

Fionn grinned. "I think we've played every session tune written to date—know O'Neill's book, backward and forward."

"Don't yez love that reel, 'St. Patrick Was A Gentleman?'" Aisling asked with fake sweetness, watching for Danu's reaction. She got one all right. Danu walked over to the back door and stepped out onto the patio, raising her arms to the sky.

"Do yez see that, lads. She *is* a druid! Still angry at St. Patrick for drivin' her sort off the island."

"Jayz, ye may be right, Aisling," Diarmuid said. Peadar's eyes were so wide his pupils shrunk to half their size. Fionn started chewing the fingernail of his right thumb.

"Grab yer stuff, lads! Let's dash out the front door while she's channeling her inner goddess," Aisling said as she jumped out of her chair and reached for her button accordion case. The moment she did, the two dogs leapt up from the door, surrounded her and snarled at her feet.

Danu walked back inside. "Where are you going? You can't leave before the session."

"I was going to warm up the accordion for our practice, right lads?"

"But why are you heading toward the front of the house?"

"I'm a bit shy," Aisling said, batting her eyes. "It's me method."

Diarmuid snorted. Aisling glared at him.

"Let's all sit down for a nice cup of tea before we practice. Come on, Aisling. Back to the table."

They sipped the herbal tea she served them. It had an odd, medicinal taste to it with hints of fennel and ginger. Next thing they knew, they were in the old Quaker meeting house, instruments ready to begin the session. None had any recollection of how the band got there.

Folding chairs had been set up in a circle on the hardwood floor. There was a side table filled with tea breads and cookies. A large pot simmered with boiling water for anyone who wanted a cup of tea.

The other musicians straggled into the hall. They smiled at

Danu then gave a cold glance toward Fionn and his band. Several of the women had long gray hair, either swept into a bun or braided down their backs. Most of the men had beards and wore flannel shirts. There wasn't an unnatural fiber in anything they wore. Aisling noticed that they all had very pink cheeks, and she surmised it was either from healthy country living or the fact that their homes had little heat. Danu stoked the wood stove earlier and the room was toasty and very dry, so much so that Fionn dampened his bodhrán with a little bit of tea water for fear its goatskin might split.

A balding man with a salt and pepper beard came in last, accompanied by a black-haired woman who looked fresh out of college. They sat next to each other and she helped him take his down jacket off.

"Nice to see a father and daughter enjoyin' the tradition of music together," Peadar said warmly to them. Faye, the young woman with the mandolin, looked at the older man and then scowled at Peadar.

"He's my lover, not my father. Josiah heads the anthropology department at the state university."

Peadar turned scarlet. Diarmuid snickered. Fionn shook his head.

"Don't you folks say, 'do not judge lest ye be judged'?" said an older woman with a hooked nose and a bun so tight it raised her eyebrows. Peadar put his head down and said a couple of Hail Marys to himself.

"'Harvest Home,' then?" Danu announced to the others as they started their moribund interpretation of the old tune. The notes were all there perfectly, but Fionn noticed they had about as much life in them as week-old boiled cabbage. These eejits are missin' the point of traditional music, Fionn thought. He looked at their dour faces and shook his head. Let's liven' up the place. Once they hit the bridge for the tenth time, Fionn flashed a broad grin, stood up and launched into a swift slip jig called "The Kid On The Mountain." His bandmates caught his fire and traded riffs with each other, laughing and winking. Aisling was rocking her head like she was at a death metal concert. The floor beneath them was bouncing up and down from their feet keeping time.

"Whoo!" Diarmuid said as he strummed his guitar so fast that Peadar broke into a sweat trying to keep up on the uilleann pipes.

"Fair play to ye, Diarmuid!" Fionn yelled. He threw his head back and grinned. "H'upyaboya!"

When they neared the end of the tune, Josiah snagged the melody and fiddled it right into the start of "Drowsy Maggie." Danu plucked the harp with the heavy cadence of an old, slightly out of tune, spinet piano. The dour faces returned and the flaming energy that Fionn's playing fanned, deftly extinguished. He looked around the room at lifeless eyes and fingers tapping instruments with the enthusiasm of a stenographer transcribing traffic court testimony. Diarmuid played the Em to D chord changes with an uninspired up-and-down strum. Aisling's button accordion wheezed along with the chord changes. Peadar had simply stopped playing, and Fionn could see he was waiting for a break in the music to launch into something to shake up these homely arts folks. He blew an opportunity when Josiah seemed to pause, because in a split second he'd already steered the players into the "Kesh Jig." Fionn thought that if anyone tried to dance to the tune at the speed they were playing it, they'd fall over because they'd have one leg up in the air and would topple over.

"This is hell," Diarmuid muttered to Aisling.

"Tell me about it." She rolled her eyes and wheezed out a G chord to a D chord to a G, D and back and forth, back and forth.

When Josiah and the other musicians hit the end of the B part (on the *sixth* time around), Fionn yelled out, "The Flogging Reel" and his band followed gleefully. The reel was apparently not in the repertoire of the session group and they sat there frowning, listening to the melody before they tried to play it. Just as they were about ready to jump in, Fionn yelled out "Martin Wynne's No. 3!"

"Whoop!" Aisling yelled as she stomped her feet like a set dancer. Diarmuid looked at her face aglow from the music and felt a pang in his heart. Och, she looks deadly gorgeous, he thought. What a brood of trad musicians they could raise together.

Peadar's eyes were closed as his uilleann pipes transported him to his "trad zone," a happy place where all he could feel was music pulsing around him. At this moment, thoughts of the wrecked car, hungry coyotes and throbbing ankle were far, far away. Trad music! Jayz, he could live on this stuff alone, it fed his soul so. Trad music and his Ma's apple cake—they made the world perfect.

"The Cloone Reel!" Fionn shouted and Slí na Fírinne danced lithely down the true path of trad music. Fionn tossed his head back and savored the brilliance of the moment. The four musicians were so tuned into each other that no eye contact was necessary. They were running on pure musical instinct.

Josiah stood up and pushed back his chair, shriek-squeaking it across the hardwood floor.

"Stop it! Stop that tune. Stop this *bullying*! You have no respect for the tradition of a session," Josiah yelled.

Fionn and the group set down their instruments. "Beg yer pardon, lad? What do ye mean?"

"You may be from Ireland," Josiah sneered, "but you know nothing of how a true session is run." Diarmuid snickered, then let his laughter roll out. Peadar cringed, oh dear Lord, not another incident in the making.

"Are ye talkin' about a true traditional Irish music session?" Aisling asked, raising her eyebrows.

"Of course, you cretin. What type of music do you think we've been playing!"

Faye patted Josiah's arm and shook her head. "We're in a Quaker meeting house. Show respect. Be peaceful."

"Yes," Danu said as she set down her Celtic harp. "Let's play nicely with each other."

"They're the ones who need to be peaceful," Josiah said folding his bow and fiddle across his chest, his lower lip trembling. "When I was studying with Seán MacLalor in Sligo, he stressed the importance of letting everyone take a turn leading a tune, to foster a sense of musical community. You have heard of Seán, haven't you? He's only the most respected fiddler in the international community," Josiah said, wireframe glasses sitting low on his nose as he glared at Fionn.

"Of course we've heard of that pompous pain in the arse!" Diarmuid said, shaking his head with a hearty laugh.

Josiah's face caught fire. "How *dare* you cast such a vulgar epithet upon an artist whose fiddle you aren't fit to tune!"

"Calm down, Josiah," Faye said, eyebrows raised. "Did you forget to put some sandalwood oil on your 'third eye' again? You know how it represses your anger."

"Don't tell me how to deal with my *anger*, woman!"

Aisling giggled. Fionn shot her a wary look. She couldn't help herself and tried to hide behind her accordion.

"You laugh at tradition," Josiah said, face even redder. "Well you're a stain on the linen of traditional Irish music."

Diarmuid guffawed.

"Ah, shite and onions," Peadar said as he looked away from the musicians. "Here we go."

"Listen ye, ye folk music nazi!" Diarmuid said. "Ye couldn't play yer way out of the Irish washerwoman's tub! What a feckin' wanker." The others couldn't help but laugh. Josiah pointed at him with his bow, as if it were a fencing foil.

"Come say that to me right here, you dumb mick!"

Diarmuid stood up and slung his guitar around his back. "Give me yer best shot, Mr. Folk Nazi!"

As Josiah lunged with his bow, Aisling grabbed a tea bread from the table behind her and threw it at him. It missed and knocked Faye in the face.

"Why you tinker tramp!" Faye screamed as she held up her mandolin like a Major League Baseball player. "Try that again!"

"Stop it! Stop it! You've desecrated this house of peace!" Danu yelled. "Diarmuid, get out of here. And the rest of you! I don't ever want to see you again!"

The four saw a bright white flash and then nothing. They

woke up in a hay field along the same country road they'd walked down toward the parade.

"What the feck happened?" Aisling said as she stood up and brushed bits of hay off her jacket.

Peadar looked scared. "Ye were right. She *was* a witch."

"And none of yez would believe me!" Aisling looked at Fionn. The lads looked down at their feet and mumbled apologies to her. Aisling folded her arms and grinned. "Where to now, fearless leader?"

"We're pointing the same direction we were yesterday, toward the sun. Let's keep going this way."

It was even warmer than yesterday, and Diarmuid pulled out a handkerchief to mop his sweaty brow before they started their march. Peadar blessed himself, and just then a van drove past. The driver slowed down and stopped, waiting for them to catch up.

"Hey there," the woman called out to them. "Do you kids need a ride somewhere?"

"That would be grand," Fionn said.

"Where are you heading?"

"We're not quite sure. We're musicians from Ireland, and we had a car accident a few days ago and now we're lost."

"Faith 'n' begorra, me own kind just walking along the highway. Get in kids."

The four opened the van doors. Fionn sat in the front seat and the rest in the back.

"Hi all, I'm Peggy O'Neill. You know, just like the song."

"The song?" Peadar asked.

"You don't know 'Peggy O'Neill'? I thought you kids said you were all Irish."

"Maybe ye could teach it to us," Fionn said, fearful of triggering another melee in this town. The woman sang the Tin Pan Alley waltz with a shrill warble. Diarmuid clawed at the window, out of her line of vision.

"Lovely song," Fionn smiled.

"So, where can I take you kids?"

"We're open to suggestions," Diarmuid said. The others laughed.

"Any of you hungry? I was heading to a card party at my church. Want to come along?"

Perhaps it was the mere suggestion of food, but Peadar's stomach rumbled.

"I heard that answer, son," Peggy said, smiling at Peadar in the rear view mirror. "Listen, they're all good cooks there, maybe if you play a few songs for us, they'll feed you. I'm sure there's plenty of food."

"That's very kind of ye to offer," Fionn said.

"Are ye Catholic? Do ye have a late Sunday Mass we could attend?"

"I said the name's Peggy *O'Neil*. Of course I'm Catholic. And yes, we have a seven o'clock Mass. Are you going to wait all week around here to attend it?" Peadar didn't understand her answer.

"What time is it now? Couldn't we make it tonight?"

Peggy thought he looked sober, and so did the others, but you can never tell these days.

"There isn't a Mass on Tuesday nights."

"Tuesday? *Tuesday?*" the bandmembers asked in unison.

Fionn turned around and gave them a look that they knew meant don't say another word or you'll frighten this kind woman.

"What day of the week do you kids think it is?" Peggy said, looking in the rear-view mirror.

"Och, of course it's Tuesday," Peadar said as Fionn nodded at him. "I was confused. Must be jet lag."

"What type of cards do yez play? Is it for money?" Diarmuid asked quickly, switching the subject.

Peggy snorted. "Hah! Nope. We play for spiritual cache: prizes are usually crystal rosaries, prayer books and folk Mass music CDs. That sort of thing."

"Sounds like fun," Peadar said. Aisling raised her eyebrow toward Diarmuid. He grinned back at her.

Peadar was upset. He'd missed Mass because he was under the spell of a druidess. How would he confess *this* to his parish priest back home? And what about that full day of missed time? Had they been hypnotized and she'd used them for one of her heathen rituals? He might have committed a mortal sin but didn't know it. Och, what would his Ma think? At least they'd be playing for Catholics tonight. Perhaps that could be the start of his penance for untold sins.

The card party was in the basement of Holy Martyrs Parish. When the musicians followed Peggy into the hall, their eyes were assaulted by forty shapes of shamrocks, from balloons to sparkly centerpieces, sea foam-green cookies to the bobbing headband on the woman taking tickets.

"They're with me, Evelyn," Peggy said. "These kids are from Ireland. Thought Annemarie might enjoy some real Irish music."

"Oh. You play music?" Evelyn said. "Silly me, I can see you have your instruments with you. Won't this be a treat?"

Peggy flagged down Annemarie as she was running around the room seeing to all the last minute preparations. She asked if the musicians could eat with them in exchange for a mini-concert. Annemarie followed her over to meet the band.

"You can stay if you promise me you'll play 'Galway Bay' because that's where my grandparents came from."

"Did they sail hookers?" Peadar asked. The woman gave him an odd look.

"Let me translate," Fionn said. "A hooker is a fishing boat often used in Galway Bay." Annemarie's face softened and she smiled.

"What a strange name for a boat."

"Ye should see what they catch," Diarmuid winked. Annemarie smiled slightly as she thought he was a bit odd, but the others looked harmless.

"Would you be able to play a half-hour's worth of music? I brought my niece's dance CD. Some Irish singer named Paddy MacSeamus."

Aisling watched Fionn's hand curl into a fist and held her breath.

"To tell you the truth," Annemarie said out of the corner of her mouth, "I think he's more Vegas than Irish." Fionn's fist unfurled and a huge smile burst upon his face. He could have kissed her. In fact, it might be a brilliant idea.

"It would be our honor to play for ye," he said, instead. "If the ladies have any other requests, we'd be happy to play them."

Annemarie clasped her hands together and smiled back. Geez, this one's cute, she thought. Too bad he looks about ten years younger.

"Well then, come have some dinner with us."

They followed her over to the buffet line where the ladies were oohing at a row of stainless steel chafing dishes just uncovered. Diarmuid sighed as the telltale scent of corned beef smacked his nostrils. Fionn glared at him and made a 'shh' gesture.

"Bet you kids are used to this cuisine," Peggy said. "It's a real treat for us. We just eat it once a year."

"That's more than me," Diarmuid whispered to Aisling. "Not anymore," she replied in singsong fashion as she started to giggle.

"Tell me, son," Peggy said to Peadar, "do you really eat potatoes all the time over there?"

Peadar looked up at the ceiling for a second as if he were doing a tally of his daily potato consumption over the past year. "Just about, Peggy."

"How do you eat them?"

"Boiled. Chips with fried fish, that sort of thing."

"My people came to America during the potato famine. Nothing personal, but I'm glad they did."

"No offense taken," Peadar smiled at her as he heaped boiled red-skinned potatoes on his plate.

After the meal, volunteers cleared the tables and desserts were set out on the buffet with a coffee and tea. Volunteers walked around posting signs on each card table indicating which game would be played there. There were tables for skat, pinochle, bridge and gin rummy.

"Could you play some instrumental music to start?" Annemarie asked Fionn. "That way the ladies can converse during their games. We play cards for an hour and a half with a fifteen minute break. You could play some lively sing-alongs during the break and at the end."

Fionn smiled at her. "That would be grand. It's the least we can do for ye after feeding us that delicious dinner. Yer husband's a lucky man." Annemarie blushed.

"Actually, I'm not married." They looked at each other for a few seconds as sly grins crossed their faces. This one's an angel, Fionn was thinking. So what difference does a few years make, Annemarie thought.

"I find it hard to believe a lovely lass like yerself isn't beating away the suitors." Fionn wasn't just handing her a compliment to make small talk. He really meant it.

"I was out of the country for more than 10 years. Worked in the Peace Corps throughout Central America. By the time I got back, all of the eligible men were taken." She shrugged her shoulders and sighed.

"Not all," he winked. She blushed even brighter. "So ye were in the Peace Corps. Wow. I'm very impressed, Annemarie. It must have been hard being away from yer homeland for so long."

"Yes, it was difficult quite often, but being in such a foreign environment—not knowing where I was half the time—did a lot to expand my appreciation of home. It gave me a true sense of gratitude for all I have, all I am."

Fionn smiled as he watched the fluorescent light play off the golden strands of her hair. She was right. Being here in America, he *was* becoming more thankful for the tradition of the music he was sharing with the world, music borne an ocean away. Annemarie felt awkward being the recipient of his stares, but really, she didn't mind it and she was slow to turn away from him.

"Well then, I see the ladies are sittin' down. We better start playin' yez some music."

Fionn and the band discussed what to play in their set. They started off with Turlough O'Carolan's "Sí Bheag, Sí Mhór" and followed it with "Eleanor Plunkett." They closed their eyes as they played, letting O'Carolan's elegant music banish their cares. Despite their exhaustion from all they'd been through, the four meshed their music into artful, aural tapestry. Fionn was thinking of Annemarie trying to find her way through the jungles of Central America and how sad it was that someone so attractive had yet to find love. Peadar was thinking how tasty those potatoes were. Aisling opened her eyes and saw Diarmuid staring at her. She grinned and he winked.

"Hey kids, thought you said you were Irish musicians?" a woman with the shoulders of a linebacker yelled. She dangled a pretzel rod off her lips like a cigar. "Don't you know any songs about whiskey?" The women in the room laughed. "Seriously, you're bringing me down with that sad stuff. C'mon, this is supposed to be a party! Give us some diddle-eye-dee stuff!"

Fionn stopped playing, and so did the others, their faces reflecting their annoyance at her outburst. He looked at Annemarie for guidance on what they should do.

"It's my fault, everyone. I told them to play some instrumental music to start," Annemarie said. "Thought you'd like to be able to talk with each other."

"Talk? Why would we want to talk with each other? Ha-ha! Give us some of them Irish rebel songs," the "linebacker" yelled. "You know, the one about stealing that guy's motorcar. Or hey, better yet, play that one about the unicorn."

Aisling saw Fionn's fist curl up again on his lap. She winced.

"Sorry, luv," Diarmuid said. "Don't know that one. But since yer 'New York Girls,' maybe yez can appreciate this one?" He jump-started the band into the lively song and soon the women were clapping as he sang "Oh you New York girls, can't you dance the polka?" When the band finished the song, they switched deftly into "Miss McLeod's Reel."

The "linebacker," whose named was Marge, got up from her table and grabbed Annemarie's arm, spinning her around so fast she became dizzy. A few other women got up and started dancing with them when the tune segued into "The Rakes of Mallow." Marge grabbed the arm of an elderly woman and pulled her out of her chair. As she spun her around, the old woman began to wheeze. Annemarie stopped Marge when it became apparent that the woman was seriously out of breath.

"Get her a glass of water. She looks like she might pass out," Peggy yelled. The band stopped as the women circled around the old woman.

Annemarie set the woman back down in her chair and asked Marge to get her a damp cloth from the kitchen.

"Can you breathe better now?" Annemarie said loudly at the woman wearing two hearing aids. She shook her head. "Are you having any chest pain?" The woman nodded.

"Argh! What a time for the phone lines to be down. Anyone have a cell phone that works? Call 911!" Annemarie gestured to the other women to back up and give the old woman some space while Marge spoke with the emergency dispatcher. "Everything's going to be OK, Mildred. Just stay calm and the ambulance will be here very soon."

"Anything I can do to help?" Fionn asked.

"Bring over a chair and help me put her legs up." He did and saw a look of terrible fear come over Mildred's face.

"Annemarie, I'm sorry but this lass is so beautiful I don't think I can concentrate on me music." Mildred grinned at Fionn. He was happy to see that he'd distracted her. "Och, I bet ye were a terror on the dance floor when ye were in yer prime," he winked at her.

"I was, young man, I *was*," Mildred said weakly. Phew, Annemarie thought, she can talk. That should be a good sign.

The ambulance arrived soon and Fionn helped the EMTs load Mildred into the back of it.

"Promise ye'll save the next dance for me, luv," Fionn said to Mildred. She took his hand and he was startled by how cold her touch was. Poor thing, he thought, her heart's so weak she's not getting enough warmth.

"I'll go to the hospital with her," Marge bellowed. "After all, it was my fault, spinning her too hard."

"Are you sure?" Annemarie asked.

"Yep. You kids have some fun. That's some killer music you play," Marge said to Fionn as she punched his arm. "Ha-ha-ha!"

Fionn returned inside, rubbing his sore arm, and saw

Peadar picking at the cold potatoes on the buffet. He looked around and didn't see Aisling or Diarmuid.

"Hey, where are the others?" Fionn asked.

"They said something about going outside for a walk. Aisling seemed very upset by the commotion."

Fionn walked out the back exit and looked around. They weren't out there. Strange. When he went back in the door, Annemarie came over to him.

"Well, what shall we do now? Let them play cards without the music? Call it a night?"

"Ye could ask them what they'd like. We can do whatever ye want, Annemarie." When she smiled at him, Fionn felt his heart leap inside. Her ash blond hair curled like flower vines around her delicate face. She looked too fragile to survive in a sweltering Central American jungle, but he sensed she had an inner strength that got her through it. He guessed it was probably faith.

"Attention everyone, the EMTs think Mildred will be just fine after a few tests at the hospital. So then, after what just happened, what do you want to do? Go ahead and play games or just chat? Do you want to hear more music?"

The women whispered to each other for a few minutes then one spoke up.

"I think their wild music would be inappropriate, but I don't think a few rounds of cards would hurt us."

They sat back at the tables and started to play their card games. Fionn shrugged at Annemarie.

"Wild musicians, the lot of us." She laughed at his comment and pushed his arm playfully. He just about died. Fionn moved close behind her as they watched the card party begin. "Ye know, I think they could get pretty raucous. Ye'll have to keep a close eye on them women," he said in a low voice that resonated on her back. She leaned back toward him for a few seconds, then turned around. "I think you may be right. So ... will you be taking off then?"

"Well, I guess, but we've no place to go." He was hoping Annemarie might extend an invitation.

"Wish I knew of a place that could take in four people on short notice," she said. "If we were in Central America, it would be no problem. People were very hospitable to travelers. Say, I wonder if Father Jerome would let you stay here at the rectory? Let me go ask."

Peadar packed up his uilleann pipes as Fionn stashed his fiddle in its case.

"Did Diarmuid and Aisling say where they were going?"

"No," Peadar said. "I figured they'd just go down the road a wee bit."

"It's getting dark out there. Hope they don't get lost."

As soon as he said that, Diarmuid and Aisling returned with sly smiles on their faces.

"Where have yez been? I was gettin' worried."

Diarmuid winked at Aisling.

"Just up the road a way," she said, "a good stretch of the legs."

"Yez shouldn't be goin' off on yer own like that. We need to stick together, all right?"

They all nodded.

"So, what's the grand scheme now?" Diarmuid asked.

"Annemarie's checkin' to see if the good father has room for us here at the rectory."

She returned looking serious. The pastor was out, she explained. There was nothing she could do. The band talked for a few minutes about what their options were.

"Should we try to walk back to Mick's place?" Peadar asked.

"Ugh, I bet the puke is still on the floor of the jacks." Aisling cringed.

"Should we try to sneak into the Murphys basement and get our suitcases?" Everyone looked at Diarmuid as if he had suggested they sleep in the middle of the road. "Or, we could see if Danu's in a better mood."

"Jaysus, are ye daft? We'd never get away from her if we went back there."

While they debated, the parish women finished their card games and tidied up the room. Fionn nibbled his right thumb fingernail. Annemarie looked over at them, felt bad, but then she had an idea.

"I just thought of someone who could help you. He's a professor at the university. Maurice often takes in foreign students before they find apartments near campus. Let me drive up there and see if he has room for you."

Fionn sighed as he watched her walk away. He hoped that maybe she'd end up offering to put them up and then, well, you know, they could see if there was something more to their mutual attraction. He wondered if maybe this was part of his price to pay for the whole Renny thing. God was sayin', "Here's a grand girl for ye, but sorry, lad. Ye can't have her 'til yer fully repented."

Meanwhile, Peadar was noticing how Aisling blushed when Diarmuid talked with her. Something was definitely up with them two, he thought.

Annemarie returned a few minutes later all smiles. "Great news. He has room for three of you. Perhaps Aisling could stay with me?"

Aisling looked at Diarmuid and frowned. Fionn didn't like the sound of that arrangement. After all, it was his responsibility to get these three back to Ireland safely. He didn't like the idea of the group being split up, especially after the weird events of the previous night.

"We appreciate his kind offer," Fionn said to Annemarie, "but I think it's best if we stay together." *You could invite me to stay with ye, however, and I'd gladly accept,* he thought. No reaction. *Why couldn't this woman be a mind reader like that Danu? Just his feckin' luck.*

"OK," she said, looking down at her feet. "I can understand that."

"Wonder if there's a barn up the road with some bales of hay we could sleep on tonight," Diarmuid said, a bit dramatically, hoping it could spur a better solution from Annemarie. "Nuthin' like a good bale of hay to catch some z's."

"You can't sleep like animals outside," she said. "Let me drive you up to Maurice's place and once he's met you, see what else he can offer."

Peggy noticed the band's long faces and came over. "Something wrong?"

"We were just trying to figure out where we'll be spending

the night," Peadar said.

"That's a pity, I know a place that's real nice and warm but I suppose it's too out of date for you." Peggy winked at him saucily and he blushed bright red. She sighed at Peadar and carried dirty dishes into the kitchen. He stood there flummoxed, eyes as big as baking potatoes.

"Looks like ye've got a live one there, boyo. Go fer it, I'd say," Diarmuid said as he patted Peadar on the shoulder.

"Robbing the grave again, are ye?" Aisling teased.

"Will yez two give it a bloody rest!" Peadar said, hands on his hips.

Annemarie said goodnight to the volunteers and returned with her coat and purse, signaling for them to follow her to the car.

"I'll explain to Maurice that you need to stay together after all you've been through. He can stay in the spare bedroom at my house tonight."

Jaysus, *no*, that's not what I was thinkin', Fionn scratched his head and frowned. He started to wonder, why would this fella be so eager to leave his house to total strangers? Is he a former boyfriend or her current lover? Och, I've blown it again! Penance, penance! He walked silently as he thought, how long until I've paid me price?

"Maurice and I know each other from our time in the Peace Corps," she said as if she were reading Fionn's mind. It startled him and he began to wonder if she did have Danu's skills. "I'm sure that I can convince him this is an emergency."

"Brilliant. To be honest, I do prefer a real bed to hay," Diarmuid said.

They squeezed into Annemarie's sedan and went off down the road humming "The Gypsy Rover." She turned the car onto a dark side road, winding and hilly. At the summit was a geodesic dome, the lights within glowing eerily against the dark countryside.

"That's a house?" Aisling asked.

"Maurice is a huge Buckminster Fuller fan. The house is completely self-sufficient. It's solar-powered, has a spring-fed water supply and he used hay bales in the construction so it's the perfect temperature year-round."

"This place looks like somethin' outta 'Close Encounters of the Third Kind,'" Peadar joked. On cue, they hummed those five "Welcome, aliens," notes.

Maurice leaned against the doorway waiting for them to get out of the car. A lanky, middle-aged man, he wore faded jeans that sagged off his thin frame. Fionn surmised he hadn't eaten a good bit of beef in a few decades. Their host waved at them and scratched his salt and pepper beard that matched the pilled wool sweater he wore. Aisling noticed when she shook his hand after being introduced, that his fingers were weathered and knobby like a blackthorn stick. Must be the price he pays for this self-sufficiency, she thought.

"Come in, come in," he said. "Let me show you around the place." Annemarie called him aside and whispered as the band entered his house.

The walls were a warm pumpkin color with a stucco-like texture. He'd built screens separating the downstairs rooms out of woven strips of recycled aluminum cans. Every bit of space was utilized to its maximum potential. A small staircase led to his office loft in a back corner. Bed frames in the rooms below were extensions of the walls. He'd also created coves with plaster shelves to hold the hundreds of books in his collection. They served literally as insulation.

"I love the design," Aisling said to Maurice and Annemarie. "So creative."

"Thank you. Being up here on this hilltop, with nothing around at night except the Milky Way above and the coyotes rustling through the woods below, clarifies your vision," he said. Maurice looked at her as if he knew that she had the gift, that is, the psychic ability passed down on the female side of her family for generations.

Aisling fingered the lapels of her jacket. "Coyotes are in the woods here? Are we safe?"

"Well, I wouldn't wander outside at night alone, but you should be safe." He laughed as he saw Peadar's eyes grow even wider than Aisling's. "Actually, those coyotes are very shy and it's easy enough to make them skitter off by creating noise or throwing rocks. Those that aren't ruffled by the commotion are probably sizing you up to see if you'd put up much of a fight if they attacked you." Aisling made a mental note of that, in case such a situation arose in the future.

He showed them where the herbal tea and a canister of homemade pumpkin seed granola were for their breakfast, in case they woke up before he returned tomorrow morning.

"Well, good night folks. Don't let the coyotes bite, hah!" he said as he draped his arm around Annemarie and headed toward her car.

"Safe home, Annemarie," Fionn said meaning watch out for that one when ye get back. She smiled and Fionn fought the urge to grab her away from that shaggy professor.

"Thanks a million, Maurice," Diarmuid yelled to him as he closed the front door.

Fionn observed the body language between Annemarie and Maurice carefully as he peeked out the front window. Was Maurice's gesture just an expression of friendliness or was there something more serious between them? When the band spread out to claim their spots for the night, he got his answer. Right next to Maurice's bed was a photo of Annemarie hugging him on a tropical beach at sunset. The pale blue waters behind them matched the color of Annemarie's sparkling eyes. Great, he thought. What if their love reignites because of tonight? What a feckin' eejit I am, he thought as he pondered yet another missed opportunity with a girl.

"Ye know, I'm going to have a nightmare that I'm trapped inside a mushroom," Peadar called out from under his blankets on the couch.

"Yeah, and there's a pack of hungry coyotes gnawing at ye," Aisling said.

"Or a leprechaun pissin' on ye." They all groaned at Diarmuid.

"Does yer Mam know what a disgustin' son she has there, lad?"

"Fionn," Diarmuid called out from his bed, "have ye tried yer mobile again?"

"Good idea there. Hold on." Fionn grabbed his coat and pulled the phone out of his pocket. When he opened it up, the screen was black. "Nope. Still dead. Wonder if our friend Maurice has a phone we could use?"

"It's probably a recycled can attached to a string," Diarmuid chuckled. Everyone looked around their space but no one found a phone.

"He must be usin' a mobile," Fionn said. "But I'd be surprised if he's gettin' a signal out here."

"Lovely. If them starving coyotes get hungry tonight and start gnawing at the wall, we won't be able to call for help. Right?" Aisling asked.

"Don't worry luv. Just scream out me name and I'll crawl over and fall on top of ye again." Diarmuid popped over the wall separating his bedroom from Aisling's and waved at her. She tossed a pillow at his face.

"And if he's still asleep, call out me name," Fionn said half kidding, half not. "Right then, let's all try to get some sleep here."

"Can ye leave a light on somewhere? It's so dark out," Aisling said. Fionn flicked a switched but it was connected to all the lights. Apparently, Maurice liked total light or darkness, nothing in between.

Soon they fell into deep sleep, probably the best they'd had since the night before the car accident. That lasted until about four in the morning, when the first hints of dawn warmed the chilly horizon. Coyotes pawed the ground outside the house, whining and yipping at each, their noise waking the four slightly, but then weaving into their dreams.

Peadar dreamed that he was lost in a giant mushroom forest. A drunken leprechaun saw him and asked for some euros so he could buy a pint. Peadar put his hands in his pockets and found he had only American pennies.

"Yer money's no good here," the leprechaun said as he frowned, folded his arms and vanished, making Peadar feel even more lost. He started to whimper in his sleep.

Diarmuid heard his crying but interpreted it in his dream as coyotes nudging the walls of the house right by Aisling's bed. He went outside to scare them away, but one wasn't afraid of him and started to come closer as if it were stalking him. Diarmuid looked around for something he could grab to scare the coyote away. He saw a stick by his feet and when he bent down to grab it, the coyote shape-shifted into Danu. She cackled at him as she floated above him, playing her harp and flashing canine teeth oozing blood.

Diarmuid, still asleep, bolted upright in his bed and yelled "No!"

Aisling heard his cry and started saying "No!" too as Maurice dragged her into a fancy room where she was surrounded by a group of well-dressed women. They were all holding up magnifying glasses at her as they whispered to one other. Aisling glanced at her hands and realized her skin had turned Kelly green. She pulled at her hair because she was nervous and saw it was green too. The women started to shake their heads. What happened to her, Aisling thought. Had she become an alien?

One of the women rang a bell and a man dressed in a white tuxedo came over, took her by the arm and escorted her outside. She could hear the derisive laughter of the women inside as the door slammed behind her. It was so dark out and Aisling felt completely helpless. She heard whining coyotes race out of the woods toward her and tried to move away from them in the darkness, but she couldn't see them or anything else. Soon they were so near she could feel their warm breath on her legs. The dream was so fearful that Aisling woke up, but her body was still in a state of sleep paralysis and she couldn't move a limb or utter a sound.

Fionn dreamed that he was lost in a Central American jungle. He could see a glint of something golden up ahead and hacked the foliage back with a machete as he walked toward it. Sunlight filtered through the banana leaves above, making the object ahead glow against the verdure surrounding it. As he neared, he realized the golden light drawing his attention was shining off Annemarie's blonde hair. She looked deadly gorgeous, wearing a skin-tight army camouflage uniform and a red beret as she pointed an AK-47 assault rifle at some weird dogs with faces like that folk nazi Josiah from the session.

"Quick! Eat some of these mushrooms," she yelled to Fionn as he approached. "They make your body give off a scent that repels the beasts."

He squatted on the jungle floor at the base of a banana tree and picked some of the red mushrooms. The beasts snarled at him, saliva dripping as they pawed the ground.

Fionn chewed a mushroom and felt a gag reflex as he realized it tasted like corned beef. He tried a green mushroom, and it tasted like boiled cabbage. "These are the strangest mushrooms I've ever tasted," he said to Annemarie.

"Shut up and just keep eating them," she yelled, pointing her rifle at the folk nazi dogs.

He shoved a handful into his mouth and as soon as he swallowed them, the beasts began to turn their noses away from him and ran off yipping as if they were injured. Suddenly, Fionn saw the dark form of Maurice swoop down from the treetop on a vine. He reached out his arm and scooped up Annemarie, then they disappeared into the jungle vegetation overhead.

When daylight broke, the band members straggled out to the kitchen one by one. All of them had dark bags under their eyes, as if they hadn't slept since their childhood. Fionn yawned while he put the kettle on the boil. Peadar stood in front of the open refrigerator, pondering its contents.

"Look at this, all he's got in here are mushrooms and soy milk!"

Fionn spun around. "Let me see that!" When he saw the wild mushrooms, it triggered a vivid recollection of his dreams the night before.

"That there's too spooky!" Fionn backed away as if he'd seen his own ghost.

"Huh?" Peadar said.

"Just an odd dream I had last night," Fionn said.

"Dream? Ye were lucky. I had a feckin' *nightmare!*" Diarmuid said as he stirred soy milk into his tea.

"Me too!" Peadar said. "Somethin' awful!"

"I was paralyzed and couldn't move, couldn't scream and the coyotes circled me," Aisling said. "It was terrifying." Diarmuid instinctively went over to her and gave her a hug. The other two raised their eyebrows at the first public display of what they'd suspected, romance was most certainly brewing between Diarmuid and Aisling.

"Do yez think it's the design of this house?' Aisling asked. "It might be tapping into some negative energy," she said looking up at the domed ceiling.

"It was negative, all right. Conjured up Danu in me dream." Diarmuid grimaced.

"That reminds me," Aisling said as she backed away from his embrace. "Ye lads never told me if yez remember what happened that night at her house."

They shook their heads.

"We're stuck in a feckin' vortex of weirdness," Diarmuid laughed.

"Och, there's druidry afoot," Peadar said."That's fer sure."

FÁINNE #5

"I trust you all slept well?" Maurice asked with a smirk when he and Annemarie returned that morning. Fionn resisted the urge to punch his bony face. The rest nodded but without enthusiasm.

Peadar suspected they'd been some sort of experiment for him. Had Maurice piped in air filled with hallucinogenic mushroom dust? Were there cameras recording their reactions? Meanwhile Fionn studied Annemarie's expression carefully to see if he could pick up a signal of whether anything occurred between the two last night. Jaysus, if only he'd been able to talk with her more, Fionn thought they could have had a real connection.

"So, Fionn," she said to him. "Where are you heading next?"

"Since it's only Monday, and the car won't be ready for a few more days, I guess we'll have to stay somewhere nearby."

"Will you be in town until St. Patrick's Day?"

"Don't know, Annemarie. We're booked for some college gigs around upstate. If the car gets done before that, I think we'll try to make at least one." Her face exhibited the slightest bit of sadness at his words, and from that he surmised (hopefully) that nothing had occurred with the professor and maybe she had similar feelings toward him. Fionn smiled at Annemarie and thought she might have blushed.

"If your band is interested," Maurice said, "I'm speaking at the Daughters of the First Settlers luncheon today at Washington Manor, just over the hill. I think the ladies might enjoy your music. Perhaps I can get them to hire you for a small stipend that you could put toward your car repair bill."

"That'd be grand, Maurice. I appreciate yer kindness, especially for letting us stay here the night. So what do the rest of yez think? Willing to play a few jigs and reels for some nice old ladies?" They nodded.

Annemarie said goodbye to the others but stepped forward to give Fionn an awkward hug. She patted his jacket several times and he held her waist more familiarly than he should of—he didn't want to say farewell. Not yet.

"It was such a pleasure meeting you," she said.

"Och, the pleasure's been all mine," he said, releasing his grip on her slowly.

"You have an amazing talent. Never forget that. Bye-bye." He watched Annemarie get into her car and sighed, wondering if the Peace Corps ever made stops in Galway.

Just before eleven, Maurice put on his hand-knit alpaca sweater and matching Peruvian hat. They followed him out the door and down the other side of the hill with their instruments to Washington Manor. Peadar's weak ankle began to throb from the pressure added to it by walking down the steep slope. Fionn noticed his struggle and offered to carry the case for his pipes. Although Peadar appreciated the gesture, he'd planned to suffer in silence like a barefoot pilgrim climbing St. Patrick's mountain—Croagh Patrick—back in Mayo. It was Peadar's idea of appropriate self-induced penance for missing Sunday Mass.

They entered a hamlet below filled with stately homes. At the edge of town stood an impressive mansion built in the Second Empire architectural style, its French-like flourishes a marked contrast to the Victoriana surrounding it. There was a wrought iron fence enclosing the elegantly landscaped property. Its massive front gates were open and they walked through them and up the bluestone sidewalk. From the front steps they could see a hint of the grandeur inside through parted lace curtains on the 12-foot high front windows.

An elegant woman wearing a hounds tooth wool suit with black velvet piping greeted them at the entrance.

"Good afternoon, Maurice. You brought guests, I see. Were we expecting them? Are they fellow professors?"

"Hello, Velma. Actually, this is a group of musicians from Ireland. Their car is in the shop and they stayed with me last night. I was wondering if you wanted them to play some Irish tunes for your luncheon today?"

Velma ran her fingers through her lavender gray hair as she squinted at the band.

"I'll have to ask the others, Maurice. They don't have any of those loud guitars with them, do they?" Diarmuid shook his head. "Well, I don't recall that we've ever had musicians of this sort in here before. Let me ask Helen if it would be appropriate."

She walked away at a measured gait leaving them standing in the ornate foyer. Peadar gawked in awe at the multi-tiered crystal chandelier overhead. Aisling counted the blossoms in a huge bouquet of spring tulips arranged in a large ormolu vase.

"They're not fake," she said as she touched them. "That's a

bleedin' fortune, right there."

Diarmuid leaned in for a closer look at an oil painting of a fox hunt hung over a mahogany Phyfe-style sofa in the sitting room. He snickered.

"*Jaysus*, I'm not in feckin' Salthill anymore," he muttered.

"Ye can say that again, lad." Fionn laughed.

Velma returned and clasped her hands in front of her.

"Yes, they can play some music as long as it isn't too loud. I'm afraid we don't have enough food to feed them, though."

"Perhaps Helen could pay them a small fee for their efforts, then?" Maurice asked hopefully.

"Well, we'll have to hear how good they are before we decide to do that," she said, staring at their wrinkled clothes.

"Ma'am, if ye don't mind. Ye've got an All-Ireland champion here on the button accordion," Fionn spoke up, pointing at Aisling. "We can play whatever sort of music ye fancy, slow airs to lively jigs." Velma smiled hesitatingly, then bid them to follow her into the dining room. They walked across vast oriental rugs, past ornate *brèche* marble fireplaces and into a spectacular ballroom with French windows from floor to ceiling.

"Not a one under 70," Diarmuid muttered as the women at the dining tables paused to look at the gypsy musicians invading their civilized repast. The tables were set with fine linens, sparkling silver, hand-cut glassware and enormous candelabras with dangling crystals that matched the chandeliers above.

"You can play over here," Velma said to the band members, pointing at an alcove next to the head table.

"Yoo-hoo, Maurice! You'll be sitting here with us," Helen,

the current president of the Daughters of the First Settlers beckoned.

The band set up their instruments and then sat on fragile-looking antique needlepoint cushioned chairs lined up against the wall. They watched silently as the women dined upon corned beef aspic, cabbage bisque and scalloped potatoes. Aisling had felt very hungry until she smelled the corned beef. Peadar was salivating as he watched the women sip soup from silver spoons. "Ye'd think they'd toss us a spare dinner roll at least," he muttered to Diarmuid.

When the women finished their lunch, waitresses cleared the tables and the women adjourned to another room where a buffet of elegant desserts, fancy coffees and Lady Grey tea awaited them. After making selections, they carried their plates back to the table and sat down for Maurice's presentation. A woman wearing an orange Chanel-style suit and a triple strand of Akoya pearls winked at the band as she carried a plate of petit fours past them.

"You're the first Irish people we've ever met," she said, running her diamond ring-heavy fingers through her hair.

"Is that so?" Fionn replied with a polite smile.

"Young man," she said leaning toward him conspiratorially, "would you *please* tell me? What *is* it about the color green?"

Diarmuid looked at Aisling, who'd already turned away from him fearing she'd giggle if they made eye contact.

"What do ye mean?" Peadar asked innocently.

"Oh, you know, don't be shy," she said as she brushed her hand across Peadar's. "All this talk about forty shades and all that," the woman said eagerly as the rest of the table laughed.

Fionn sat back in his chair and took a deep breath.

"The way I see it, ma'am, is that we're an island. And ye know, islands are apt to get a lot of rain. The more rain ye get, the greener yer landscape." The woman nodded at him as if that thought had never occurred to her, then satisfied with his answer, made her way slowly back to her seat.

Maurice began his lecture on sustainable energy and the band members were grateful to be out from under the microscopes of these probing society types. As Maurice droned on about the importance of leaving light environmental footsteps, Fionn tried to put together a playlist in his mind that would suit this audience. A waitress came over and asked quietly if any of the band members would like a drink of water.

"Thanks luv, fer yer kindness," Peadar said when she returned with tall glasses for them all.

"Come by the kitchen after the luncheon is over and I'll feed you all," the young girl whispered to him. The thought that there was food soon in his future made Peadar very happy. He smiled broadly and she winked back.

When Maurice finished his lecture (that drove more than a few Daughters of the First Settlers into an early nap time), Helen walked up to the podium with her cane, presented him with an envelope and thanked him for his astute observations on America's current energy policies.

"I understand we also have you to thank, Maurice, for providing us ladies with a special treat for this St. Patrick's Day week. He's brought along some Scottish friends who will be playing reels and jigs for us." There was murmuring across the tables and then one of the women stood up, the one with the orange suit who'd been talking with the band.

"Madame President, if you'll pardon me, I would like to correct what you just said. These musicians are from *Ireland* and we've just had the most fascinating discussion on why their country is so green." She looked at Fionn then back at the women. "It's because it's an *island* and it receives a substantial amount of precipitation in the form of rain." Women across the room repeated her words, "It's because of the *rain*."

"I stand corrected Dorothy. Now the young man who is the leader of the band, would you care to introduce yourselves and tell us a little bit about the music you'll be playing?"

"*Go raibh míle maith agaibh,*" Fionn said as he rose from his chair. "That's a thousand thanks to ye in me country's own language, Gaeilge. Me name's Fionn and I'll be playing the fiddle for yez. Next to me is Peadar on the uilleann pipes, the Irish bagpipe played with yer elbow. Diarmuid is the handsome lad on guitar and we're honored to have an All-Ireland button accordion champion with us, Aisling there, over in the corner. We're called Slí na Fírinne, or the path of truth. Our group will be playin' the traditional music of Ireland that ye'd hear in a typical pub or home. We'll start with a concerto by the blind Irish harpist Turlough O'Carolan, follow that up with a reel, a slip jig and finish with a lively set of jigs. Perhaps Maurice could pull back that oriental rug so yez can get up and dance if yer so inclined." He laughed, as he winked at the audience. The women responded with stony stares.

Fionn raised his eyebrows at the others. "Right then, *a haon, a dó, a haon dó trí....*" As soon as they started playing, they noticed how wonderful the acoustics were in the room, how they made every note brighter and richer. That spurred them to make the most beautiful music they could for this impromptu show. They sat back and relaxed when the reel switched into the slip jig. By the time they reached the jig set, their feet were bouncing on the hardwood floors and they were laughing and winking at each other. Fionn set down the fiddle and brought out his bodhrán for a complex drum solo in the second jig of the set. It was so wonderful, the other musicians gradually stopped playing to admire his virtuosity. Fionn felt like he was playing on the stage of Carnegie Hall, the music felt that brilliant.

When Fionn reached a bridge in his solo, Aisling started up the final jig in the set to close their show. They were so in the moment. They all knew that this was why they played traditional Irish music for a living. They were on a trad music high and didn't want it to end, but they knew they'd been allotted a brief half hour to play. When the final note sounded, they looked at each other and braced for thunderous applause.

The women sat there, hands folded in their laps, smiling weakly at them. What just happened? Had their playing somehow offended them, Fionn wondered. Was it too loud? What else could have been wrong with what seemed like a perfect set? There had to be some reason to receive no reaction at all.

Helen hobbled back up to the podium.

"Well, then. That concludes this month's luncheon. See you all in April."

When the women got up to leave, it was as if the band was invisible. Even the semi-friendly woman in the orange suit passed by them without the slightest glance in their direction. Diarmuid took it to heart. He felt as if they were untouchables living in the slums of Mumbai. Not one person said thanks or even smiled at them. They were just background noise to these women. It was so disheartening—they'd put their all into this performance. To get no response whatsoever was probably the worst thing anyone could have done to them. It was such an affront to the core of their being.

Maurice walked out with Helen and chatted with her about something in the foyer while the musicians were abandoned in the dining room to pack up.

"Psst! Are you guys hungry?" the waitress motioned to them from the kitchen. They carried their instruments behind the swinging kitchen door where the waitress set up some plates with food for them.

"Hi, I'm Katelyn by the way," she said as she shook Peadar's hand.

"I'm Peadar. Thanks a million, luv. I was starvin' watchin' all them ladies ate'n."

"Fat chance of those tight-ass broads tossin' you a crumb!" Her frankness startled and delighted the group and they all had a good laugh. Even though it was more corned beef, Aisling ate her meal voraciously. The texture was a bit odd, but none of them cared.

"Can't thank ye enough," Peadar said to Katelyn.

"So, you really are from Ireland?" she asked.

"Absolutely. I'm from Westport in County Mayo. The rest are from the Galway City area. Diarmuid's from Salthill, Aisling hails from Ballinfoyle and Fionn, our fearless leader is a Boyne Valley native who grew up in Clare but now resides in Galway proper. We're from the West, the best, of Ireland."

"I'd love to get over there some day. Won't happen soon on what I make here, though," she sighed.

"Well, when ye do, ring me up and I'll be yer tour guide," Peadar said, beaming at her. What a lovely girl. He wondered if she was Catholic.

"Where are you going next?"

"We're waiting for our car to be repaired," Peadar said as he grabbed a roll and buttered it. "We're in the States on a tour of upstate college campuses. Had a week of gigs booked, but after the accident, our schedule's banjaxed."

"Ban what?"

"Totally fooked," Diarmuid interrupted as he grabbed another roll, too. Peadar frowned at the interruption.

"We're like tinkers now, haven't a clue where our next meal or place to sleep will be," Aisling said as she sipped her tea.

"Really? You guys need a place to stay? 'Cause I have an apartment off, off campus, and my roommate has gone home early for the weekend. You could crash at my place tonight."

Peadar grinned and nodded. Thank ye Lord, he thought.

Maurice walked in the kitchen and looked at the band members angrily.

"There you are! I've been looking all over for you. Who said you could eat?"

The four shrugged then looked at Katelyn.

"I did," she said as she put her hands on her hips. "I was just going to toss this food out anyway."

"Well don't let Helen catch them in here. She'll have a fit!"

"Sorry, lad. We had a terrible hunger upon us."

"Here's some money from the Daughters," he said handing Fionn an envelope.

"Tell me, Maurice. Do ye think they enjoyed our show?"

Maurice looked out the window for a few seconds then smiled at Fionn.

"Well, can't say you were exactly their cup of tea, but then again, they didn't throw you out. Are you kids ready to leave?"

Peadar looked at Katelyn, then at Fionn.

"I've invited them to stay at my place tonight," Katelyn said. "I've hired them to play at my hump day, pre-St. Patrick's blowout."

Maurice shook his head. "Don't you college kids do anything these days besides getting drunk?"

Katelyn put her finger on her chin and looked up as if she was thinking. "Nope!"

"Are you sure you want to crash at some college student's apartment tonight?" Maurice frowned. "You want to give up the comfort of my home?" (And the feckin' nightmares it gives us, Aisling thought. You bet!) They all nodded that they were set to spend the night at Katelyn's place.

"All right then. Pleasure meeting you all."

"Thanks a million again for yer hospitality, Maurice," Fionn said extending his hand. "And thank Annemarie again for us, too. We'd gladly repay yez if ye ever visit Ireland."

"I'd like that," Maurice said as he shoved his Peruvian hat back on his head, yanked its dangling chin strings, and smirked out the door.

FÁINNE #6

Katelyn O'Malley lived in an apartment that spanned the third floor of a former typewriter factory. In any big city, loft space like this would be worth millions of dollars. The apartment was located in recession rife upstate New York, however, so its value was a fraction of that.

Katelyn, a local girl, studied art education at the state university about a half hour away. Her roommate was a biology major at the private university a bit farther away than that. They'd decorated their apartment eclectically with secondhand furniture and found items used as makeshift seating. None of the chairs at their dining room table matched. Katelyn painted each in different colors such as lavender, cherry pink and lemon yellow, then decorated their spindles and arm rests with checkerboard, polka dot or zebra stripe patterns. She'd hung a shower curtain with tropical fish on it as a divider between the dining room and the kitchen. Their bedrooms were separated by mismatched bookshelves lined up like cubical walls. The windows didn't need curtains since they were in the village's lone "skyscraper" and hovering helicopters weren't exactly an issue. At the far end of the room was the bathroom—the lone space enclosed completely offering a tiny oasis of privacy in the vast room.

Katelyn sat cross-legged on a giant round cushion as she

called up her friends on her cell phone to let them know about her party that evening. Fionn and the rest of the band stared out the windows at great views the apartment offered. From the corner of the building they could see the dome of Maurice's home, high atop the hill. Out the other windows was a panorama of the hamlet's main street, including the rooftop of Washington Manor. Ruddy spring buds dotted color on the otherwise gray-bare trees. It looked like a peaceful place to live, they thought.

"Ask Katelyn if ye can borrow her mobile to call Des," Aisling said, nodding at their hostess chatting animatedly, her arms making grand gestures as she described the scale of party planned for tonight.

"Why do that? Do you want to go to our gig and miss this evenin's craic?" Diarmuid said with a wink. "I have a feeling this party's goin' to be epic."

"I hope no one vomits in here," Peadar said. "Can still smell Mick's from four days ago."

"Thanks fer bringin' that up again," Aisling said as she pinched her nose.

Fionn waited until Katelyn hung up and approached her with a smile.

"I was just wonderin' if I could...."

"Damn! Look at that. My cell's dead already. Excuse me a sec. Gotta get this charged up. I have so many calls to make."

Fionn stared past her out the window. Was there no path out of this rural hell? Would he ever be able to contact his cousin or make it to any of their gigs? (Of course he'd left the gig list with contact numbers in the glove compartment of the car, now parked in a repair bay at Butch's shop.) The rest of the group seemed to be holding up, but how long before their adaptability morphed into frustration and anger?

He wished Annemarie had taken them in instead of Maurice. Maybe she could have given them a ride back to Butch's to check on his progress with repairing their car. He wondered if Brian Murphy would ever try to find them and return their belongings. He worried that Danu might be related to Katelyn, and somehow she'd show up at the party tonight. His rushing crazy thoughts were distracted by the sound of music coming from the corner. The rest of the band were settled in already, playing a lively tune. It was the "reel way" to deal with a situation that appeared beyond their control.

"I think yez need a fiddle to go with that jig," Fionn said. He opened the case, grabbed his instrument and pulled over a lavender chair to join the impromptu session.

While they were playing, Katelyn slipped out to the corner store to buy some snacks and beer. The deli had a sale on Reuben sandwiches, so she bought some and a jar of kosher dill pickles for their dinner. Fionn and the others were so into their music, they hadn't noticed that the sun set over Maurice's hill. It was getting dark out by the time Katelyn returned.

"You guys are amazing! Wait until my friends hear you," she said as she carried in arms full of groceries. Peadar set down his pipes and ran over to assist her. "There's some beer down at the bottom of the stairwell. Would you be able to get that?"

"Absolutely, luv," Peadar said as he descended the stairs, favoring his weak ankle. When he returned carrying the two cases of beer, he was winded.

"How did ye get all this here?" he asked, setting the beer on the kitchen counter.

"My shopping cart is parked out back," Katelyn said with a laugh. "This town's so small, they let me take the cart home with me. Seth's cool that way. He says maybe he'll stop by after the deli closes."

"How many people are ye expectin'?"

"You never know. Sometimes seven people will show, sometimes seventy. All depends on if there's something better on campus tonight. It's a bit of a road trip for my friends. But they know they can all crash here if they want."

Peadar looked around the space that shrank suddenly as he envisioned seventy comatose bodies joining them on the floor.

"I got us some dinner. Do you think the others are hungry yet?"

"Ye never have to ask us that," Peadar laughed.

"Hey guys! Chow time!" Katelyn yelled as she held up the bag of sandwiches. "There's beer and soda in the fridge if you're thirsty." She set five paper plates and some napkins on the table.

"What's on the menu?" Diarmuid asked.

"Reubens! Seth makes the best deli sandwiches in town. Well, actually he's the only deli in town," she laughed as she opened the pickle jar and set the wrapped sandwiches on everyone's plates.

"What's a Reuben?" Aisling asked.

"A typical deli sandwich that you have to eat with a nice juicy dill pickle. They're very popular in New York City. It's always on toasted rye bread and is dressed with sauerkraut, Swiss cheese and Russian dressing."

"Vegetarian?"

"No! How could I forget. It's got corned beef."

Aisling looked at the unwrapped sandwich in front of her. "Oh."

Katelyn noticed they all had the same disappointed look on their faces.

"Is something wrong?" she asked.

Fionn patted her shoulder. "No, we're just very grateful for yer kindness. Diarmuid, can ye pass me a beer?"

Katelyn's guests started arriving after nine in waves, Peadar noticed warily, and he kept a mental tally as he wondered where they'd all sleep. It was looking like he and the rest of the band would have yet another weird night's sleep. Bellowing voices and the sound of pop tops snapping open beer cans soon shattered the peace of the loft.

Aisling and Diarmuid chuckled as they pointed out the T-shirts the young men wore. Every guy in the loft had something distasteful to get off his chest: "St. Patrick is me homeboy," "I swear to drunk I'm not God," "Get ready to mumble,""Who's your Paddy?" "Let's get blarney stoned," and the one that particularly made Aisling's flesh crawl, "Rub me for luck."

"Will ye look at that, Fionn?" Peadar asked as he caught his attention and tsk-tsked at a guy with a shaved head chugging beer from a funnel. His shirt said "*Póg mo thóin!*"

"Indeed," Fionn nodded. "*Buíochas le Dia*, Gaeilge's not dead in America!"

Someone turned on a CD of Celtic punk that switched the

testosterone in the room to overdrive. "Oi! Oi! Oi!" the kids yelled in unison, jumping up and down like bungee cords. Peadar, wide-eyed in the corner sipping cola, imagined the floor giving way beneath them. One guy started his version of a jig, and soon the room was spinning with people locking arms and swinging around like square dancers on crack.

"*Jaysus*! This is feckin' insane," Fionn said to Peadar as they watched the lads line up around the table for Irish car bombs: shot glasses of Irish whiskey and Bailey's Irish Cream dropped into pints of Guinness and then chugged on the count of three.

"Och, there'll be a baptism of this floor with vomit tonight," Peadar said as he cringed.

"Do ya know what day this is?" one guy said as he ran up to Peadar. He shook his head.

"It's Wednesday. O'Hump Day! *Booyah!*" he said as he mimed riding a horse. Peadar grimaced and turned away.

The young men weren't the only ones drinking. Katelyn and her girlfriends mixed a batch of Emerald Isle martinis with gin, crème de menthe and bitters. The scary green beverage looked like something from a witch's cauldron, Fionn thought. Then he looked over his shoulder suddenly, wondering if Danu had joined the bacchanal.

"Hey Irish people, your band can start whenever you want," Katelyn yelled over the loud music.

"Right, then. We'll tune up now." Fionn wolf-whistled to get the attention of the others and they gathered in a far corner as Katelyn turned off the stereo.

"Hey! Whatcha do that for?" one guy with a mohawk yelled.

"Relax, you moron. We have a real band from Ireland here."

"Hah, are they gonna play some lame-ass leprechaun jigs for us?" a guy said. (He wore, ironically, a T-shirt that read: "Magically delicious.")

"Dude, do you know any drinking songs?" another young man asked as he leaned toward Fionn, almost spilling his beer on him.

"Ye know, I think we might know a few," Fionn said as they started off with a reel called "The Jug of Punch." They were surrounded by a wall of young men staring with judging eyes.

A cute coed sidled up to Diarmuid as he played. Aisling didn't appreciate the girl invading her territory, and when the girl started whispering in his ears, Aisling missed a few notes. Fionn looked up at her and she shrugged.

The tune ended and Diarmuid turned to the coed. "Sorry luv, I don't know Bono and we don't play any U2. OK? Now feck off!" Aisling laughed and Diarmuid rolled his eyes at her.

"Hey, do you guys play that song by Metallica, 'Whiskey In The Jar'?"

Diarmuid smirked as he strummed the opening chords on his guitar. "Sure, but they didn't write it."

The young man glowered at Diarmuid. "I've got their album, bro. I think I know what I'm talkin' about." He folded his arms. They were quite beefy—corned beefy—Diarmuid noted. He decided to keep his mouth shut and follow Fionn into their rendition of the requested tune.

Speed, not accuracy, set the bar of music higher with this crowd. After an hour into their playing, Fionn also realized that the faster they played, the more tired this group of drunks would get and perhaps it would expedite the end of the party. Aisling looked at him with an expression he knew meant that she was dyin' to take a break, but he kept playing. God, just get us through this night unscathed, he prayed silently.

"Hey, you guys hungry?" one guy with red hair teased into nasty dreadlocks said. "You can have some of my Pocket Sammy. Here," he said holding out a microwaved pastry oozing scary burned corned beef.

Peadar smiled politely and shook his head. "Still full from dinner," he said.

"OK, dude. But if you change your mind, I'll be by this keg."

Fionn's heart sank when he saw the young men rolling a half keg into the room. They'll be goin' strong 'til dawn, he thought. With a nod of his head, he signaled to the band to take a break. Aisling set down her accordion and dashed off to the bathroom, but the door was locked. She saw Katelyn and explained that she needed the facilities immediately. Katelyn pounded on the door and yelled "Hurry up!" Aisling blushed and looked around the room. Katelyn was impatient and rattled the door handle. Nothing.

"C'mon, there's a toilet you can use on the second floor. I'll go with you. It's a little creepy down there." When Katelyn grabbed a flashlight by the door, Aisling began to feel nervous. When Katelyn broke into the empty apartment just below her, she got scared.

"What if the *gardaí* see us in here? Won't we be arrested?"

"You mean the cops? Nah, I know most of them. Harmless as puppies. There you go. It's across the room."

Aisling followed the beam of Katelyn's flashlight and ran

across the worn hardwood floor into an unheated bathroom. She feared her body might freeze to the toilet, so she went as fast as she could. Above her, the heavy booted feet of partiers bounced the ceiling up and down to some more Celtic punk. Jayz, I hope they don't come crashing through the ceiling, she thought. She could see the headline in the papers back home: "Galway girl dies in freak jacks accident."

When they returned to the party, Aisling saw a guy with a T-shirt that said "O'Snap!" pouring beer down a funnel into Diarmuid's mouth. What the …? Her eyes darted around the room looking for the others. Fionn was dropping an Irish car bomb as Peadar sipped an Emerald Isle with his pinky out.

"I leave for a second and this is what happens," she said, not really meaning for Katelyn to hear her.

"If you can't beat 'em, I say join 'em. Come over to the bar and I'll fix you an Emerald Isle."

Peadar chatted up a group of girls at the bar. They kept asking him to say things so they could hear it with his Irish accent.

"Can you say 'You're always after my Lucky Charms'?" a cute redhead asked.

"Yer always after me Lucky Charms." Peadar grinned as they giggled.

"Say 'thirty-three and a third,'" a pretty blonde begged.

"Tirty-tree and a tird," he replied, laughing at himself. "Och, now don't hate me girls 'cause I can't pronounce me hayches." That made them giggle all the more.

"Say I'm a feckin' eejit," Aisling interrupted.

"She's a feckin' eejit," he replied, making the girls laugh

riotously. Aisling just shook her head.

"Are you in the IRA?" one asked, suddenly serious.

"No, but me mate Diarmuid is, the funnel man over there. Whatever yez do, don't get the lad angry."

They looked at Diarmuid who was having a bit of difficulty standing without swaying.

"Has he ever killed a man?" the redhead asked.

"There's talk of one time when he came home late with blood on his hands. He said he slipped on the Salthill Prom that rainy night. Others say it's no coincidence that it was the night Johnny Pat McGavin went missing."

"Peadar, yer so feckin' full of shite," Aisling said as she wandered off to explore the Emerald Isle in her hand.

"Don't listen to her," he said to his captive audience. "She's just jealous of yer beauty." Jaysus, he thought, he couldn't remember a time ever in his life when he'd been surrounded by such deadly girls (especially that Katelyn). Gorgeous! "By the way, do ye think we'll all fit here if everyone stays overnight?" he asked.

A guy wearing an "Irish Whiskey Makes Me Frisky" T-shirt was looking at Fionn's fiddle while he was distracted by some college girls across the room. The guy picked up the instrument and drew the bow across it making an awful squeak. Fionn spun around and glared at him. "Put that down, lad."

"Dunno, kinda like the way it feels under my chin. Think it makes me look even friskier."

"We get the picture and it isn't pretty. So just be a good lad there and set it back in the case."

"You sayin' I'm not pretty?"

Fionn sighed. This kid was obviously drunk and he didn't want to tangle with him. He especially didn't want anything to happen to his instrument.

"C'mon, lad," Fionn said, pointing at the fiddle case.

Mr. Frisky jutted out his chin and snipped, "I'm in the mood for a jig." He sawed away at the fiddle making horrible sounds as he mimed what looked like Michael Flatley "riverdancing" on a Tilt-A-Whirl. Diarmuid sobered quickly as he realized what was going on and circled the room so he could grab the fiddle from behind the drunk. As Fionn neared from one side, Diarmuid closed in from the other. It was like flushing game out of the woods.

"Whatsa matter, Irish dude?" the drunk said, dangling the fiddle by its neck. "You think I'm playin' better than you can? Well you won't be able to if it slips out of my ...."

Diarmuid lunged forward and caught the fiddle before it crashed to the floor. Fionn swooped in from another side and grabbed the bow out of his other hand. The drunk roared, picked up one of Katelyn's decorated chairs and flung it at the window so hard that it shattered the glass. The chair flew down three stories until it bounced off the roof of the lone police cruiser in the hamlet. Two police officers inside it had already been summoned to the property by a neighbor annoyed with the constant oi-oi-ing. By the time the officers ran up the three flights to Katelyn's apartment, a full-fledged donnybrook had erupted.

Aisling and Diarmuid stayed put in the far corner, protecting the instruments from airborne bottles of beer and other pieces of furniture. Peadar cowered under the kitchen counter with Katelyn and the other girls he'd been chatting up. Fionn's fists flew furiously matching every punch the drunk threw at him. No one noticed the cops were there until one blew a shrill whistle. Fists paused in midair. Fionn was holding the drunk out at arm's length.

"Everyone up against the far wall," Officer Mulroney yelled. "OK, you yahoos. Which one of you lives here?"

Katelyn stood up from behind the kitchen counter and raised her hand.

"Come over here for a second, miss. We'd like to speak with you." Katelyn whispered with the cops for a few minutes. She gestured toward Fionn and the drunk. Officer O'Dell approached them.

"OK, who threw that chair out the window?"

"This stupid Irish dude!" the drunk yelled, pointing at Fionn.

"Do ye think we're all blind, man? I did no such thing, ye bastard."

"Did so. Didn't he, Mitch?" the drunk said, looking at his college roommate.

"It happened so fast, officer. Biff here's pretty wasted. I doubt he'd be able to throw a chair like that."

"Yeah," another college kid chimed in. "No way Biff did that. This guy's in the IRA. Killed a man once, Katelyn said."

She pointed at him from across the room. "Shut up. Josh, you're *such* a liar. I never said that!" she said, hands on hips.

"STUPID BITCH!" Josh yelled.

Fionn spun around and punched him in the mouth. Josh whimpered. Katelyn beamed at her honor being defended by such a handsome Irishman.

-133-

"OK, Mr. Hot Potato Head," Officer O'Dell said, grabbing Fionn by the collar. "That type of behavior might be the norm in Ireland, but we don't allow it here."

"That feckin' chancer grabbed me fiddle and was going to drop it on the floor. That's me income, right there."

"I had to catch it before it fell into smithereens," Diarmuid added, as he stepped forward with the fiddle.

"Who are you? Brother or cousin?"

"Friend and band mate. We're here in the States to play some gigs at the local colleges."

"Just you two?"

"No. Aisling over there with the rest of the instruments and Peadar is ... where is he?"

"Over here!" one of the girls yelled out. Peadar stood up from behind the counter, red faced.

"Listen up kids. All of you leave except Biff, Katelyn and these Irish. I don't want any of you driving home, OK?" Officer Mulroney said as he took off his cap, scratched his head and tried to figure how he'd sort out this mess.

"Tell me again, Irish," he said, "how did this start?"

"I was talkin' with some girls and all of a sudden, I hear this awful sound comin' out of me fiddle. I look around and this *cabóg* is scratchin' at it. I asked him to stop, put it down and he didn't."

"And that's when you threw the chair at the window?" Officer O'Dell asked.

"No, listen to me. I never bleedin' touched that chair. Biff starts dancin' like a feckin' eejit with me fiddle and I'm gettin' angry like and ...."

"What type of music do you play again?" Officer Mulroney asked.

Fionn looked at him with exasperation. "Traditional Irish music. Jigs. Reels. That sort of thing."

"And who threw the first punch?" Officer O'Dell asked.

"I don't remember," Fionn said.

"You lyin', ape-faced leprechaun!" Biff yelled as he lunged at Fionn.

"Don't push yer luck there, boyo," Fionn said with a cold scowl that *did* look like he'd learned it in the IRA.

"Ever play music for Irish dancers?" Officer Mulroney asked.

"Of course, all the time." Fionn grinned slightly, this was the oddest interview he'd ever had with the gardaí.

"He prefers to play for fairies, don't you Mr. Leper Con!"

"Shut yer bloody gob, ye feckin' eejit," Fionn said.

"Make me!" Biff taunted.

"FECK OFF, *amadán*!"

"A wha...?"

"Settle down you two," Officer O'Dell said, pushing them apart. "Let's get back to the chair. Who picked it up?"

"He did. He grabbed me by the throat first, spun me around and then picked up the chair," Biff said.

"Ye bleedin' fecker, I did nuthin' of the sort!" Fionn yelled.

"See, he scratched me," Biff said as Officer O'Dell leaned in to see. He looked at Officer Mulroney and nodded.

"OK, all you Irish come over here. I want to see your passports."

Fionn, Diarmuid and Peadar took their passports out. Aisling froze, looking uncomfortable.

"How about you, Missy? Where's yours?"

Aisling turned red. "I don't have it right now."

"Did you come into this country illegally?"

"No! Of course not! Ye see, we got in this car crash and have been staying with all sorts of people around here as we've been waiting for it to be repaired. Me passport's in me suitcase, at the Murphys' house. They got mad at us because of the music we played at the Ruffed Grouse Lodge and then they kicked us out but wouldn't give us back our luggage."

"I see, so you've already got a history of causing trouble here on your visit," Officer O'Dell said as he jotted something down in a notepad.

"Murphys? Brian Murphy?" Officer Mulroney asked.

She nodded.

"He's my cousin."

Peadar and Diarmuid grimaced as they looked at Fionn.

"I can't stand his bratty, prissy daughters," Officer Mulroney said laughing. The band members smirked. "OK, all you Irish come with us. Biff, give Officer O'Dell your address and phone number. We'll be in touch."

"But officer, I swear, I *never* threw that chair!" Fionn protested.

"OK, right, the chair was mad at all the partiers and decided to take its own life?" Officer O'Dell sneered. "Go downstairs and get in the car!"

Peadar waved a weak goodbye to Katelyn as she pouted.

Och, an opportunity missed, he thought. Bet she could make a good apple cake, too. The feeling was mutual, but the timing was unfortunate. Katelyn was more upset about him being taken away than the gaping hole in her living room window. Geez, was she ever going to meet Mr. Right?

FÁINNE #7

Their first overnight stay in an American jail was surprisingly more comfortable than they'd imagined. Peadar was happy also, frankly, that he didn't have to share floor space in Katelyn's apartment with any leftover partiers.

Breakfast wasn't bad: a hot beverage, piece of fruit and choice of cereal. They ate in silence. All of them wondered where this latest turn of events would take them next. How soon would Butch be done fixing their car? Once they got sprung from jail, would they be able to get a ride over there to check its progress?

No one told them why they were all incarcerated. Diarmuid figured it was American post-9/11 mistrust of any disruptive foreigners. Their names were probably being checked against a list of IRA suspects. (Ye can tell this country was settled by British, he thought.)

Fionn knew that apartment window would be expensive to replace if they insisted that he, not Biff, busted it. Perhaps they could offer to play a gig or two to raise money for Katelyn, he thought. After all, she'd been very kind to them.

Around 11 a.m., Officer Mulroney finally stopped by to speak with them.

"We're going to release you kids after lunch, we think. One of the college kids called from campus to say it was Biff who threw the chair out the window. He's coming down after his class to make a statement. You'll have to stay around town for at least 24 hours in case we have any more questions." They all nodded at the officer. Aisling was happy. She was so worried that she'd face criminal charges for being in the country illegally because she didn't have her passport.

"You kids have any plans for this evening?"

Diarmuid smirked. Fionn frowned at him and he stopped it.

"No officer," Fionn said. "No plans."

"You see, I'm asking because the wife does Irish dancing, you know that sevens and threes stuff. They have practice on Thursday nights in the Grange Hall. Any chance you kids could play for them tonight?"

Fionn was eager to stay on Officer Mulroney's good side. "We'd be happy to play for them," he said, although inside he was dreading a possible encounter with more Paddy MacSeamus fans. "What time? Where's the hall?"

"They practice at 6:30. The Grange Hall is across the street from Seth's Deli. Not far from that apartment you were in."

"Right. We'll be there."

After they were released, Fionn and the group walked down the street toward a creek-side park with a picnic area and playground. It was a sunny day, luckily, and it was even warmer than yesterday. Peadar took off his jacket, folded it into a tidy pillow and napped on the picnic table bench as Diarmuid pushed Aisling on a swing.

"Ye know I've got the gift, Diarmuid? Inherited it from me Grandma Maggie."

"What's it like? Do ye see dead people?"

Aisling laughed. "Nooo, nuthin' like that. It's far more subtle. These feelings come over me all of a sudden. Usually I shrug them off, but when I pay attention to them, I realize they're messages from spirit guides."

"Do they ever say things like, fall in love with the guitar player in yer band?" Diarmuid couldn't believe the words tumbled out of his mouth. No way of taking them back now.

Aisling punched his arm playfully. "Yer a bold one, Diarmuid. Foxy-bold. What would yer friend Eamon say back home if he knew ye were hittin' on his girl at this moment?"

"Fair play to ye, lad. I couldn't figure that girl out at all. It's like me sixth sense was tellin' me, och she's better off with me mate Diarmuid."

"In yer dreams, Kinsella!" Aisling laughed pumping the swing higher and higher. The jolly look on her face changed suddenly and she stopped the swing and looked behind her toward the creek.

"What is it, girl? Is yer gram tellin' ye somethin' now?"

"Up on the table! Now." She ran over to the picnic table and hopped on it. Diarmuid ran after her, laughing. "What the feck's the matter, lass?"

"There's a snake over there."

"Where?"

"On that rock, by the creek."

"So ye've got a sixth sense and a snake sense. Lotsa talent, there."

Fionn wandered over to the creek past the snake sunning

itself and watched the stream gurgle over ridges of shale. There was a small pool under a mini-waterfall where he watched sunlight reflect off silvery minnows. He chewed the fingernail of his right thumb as he pondered how he could get his band out of this mess. A small bass floated by and when it got right near him, flipped out of the water for a brief moment, wagged its tail fin at him, then floated downstream.

That's it, Fionn thought. We'll put on a St. Patrick's Day show on to raise money for our car and travel back to Boston. But where? What venue would be suitable? Not the Ruffed Grouse Lodge. Definitely not Washington Manor. This Grange Hall they were going to tonight might be suitable, but how would they get liquor there? A place with liquor would be better for a party atmosphere and quick money raising. A restaurant or pub is what they really needed.

Fionn joined the group 'round the picnic table and told them his plan. It sounded as good as any idea to them. "Where are ye plannin' this gig?" Diarmuid asked.

"Be on the lookout for a suitable pub, restaurant or banquet facility. A place with a dance floor and drink."

"Let's figure out a playlist, then," Fionn said. They got out their instruments and had a pickup practice session. Fionn asked Aisling if she'd care to sing some *seán-nós* songs in Irish. That'd be really different for the folks around here. Diarmuid knew most of those rebel songs. Nuthin' like 'em to get the crowd goin'. He wanted Peadar to play the songs people associated with highland pipe bands, songs with a high emotional factor such as "Amazing Grace" and "The Minstrel Boy." They spent the rest of the afternoon practicing their music. About six o'clock, a police cruiser pulled up.

"You kids need a lift to the Grange Hall?" Officer Mulroney called out to them from his car.

"Absolutely," Fionn said as they crossed the park to get into the car. It was a short ride down the street. The building was a simply framed stucco structure with a basement and first floor, both offering good-sized kitchens, dance floors and stages.

When the band walked inside, they met dancers dressed in clothes you'd see on residents of the Aran Islands in the Fifties. The women wore red wool skirts with black shawls crisscrossed over their white blouses. The men had on white shirts and dark pants tied with a red and white *crios* (a handwoven Aran Islands belt). A woman slipped an album of set dance music into the CD player. Fionn recognized the playing style as from the Doonmacdubh Céilí Band of County Clare. Jaysus, at least these folks have some taste, unlike those Murphy girls, he thought.

Officer Mulroney went over to his wife Shayla and told her about the musicians. He made it sound as if he'd just met them in the park, not that he'd jailed them overnight. Shayla smiled and scurried over to greet them.

"I like yer taste in music, Mrs. Mulroney," Fionn said.

"Oh, we like them, too. I bought that at the feis in Syracuse. Can you play music for céilí *and* set dances?"

"Of course. They're all reels, jigs, polkas and hornpipes. That's what we specialize in."

"Oh, that would be wonderful. What a treat to have live music!"

One of the male dancers came over to meet the band and

Shayla introduced his as Ned, the leader of the Kennedy Céilí Dancers. He wore an ill-fitting black toupee that matched his oily, pencil-thin mustache creating the effect of a Celtic carnival barker.

"Nice to meet you. Say, have you ever competed at the *Fleadh Cheoil na hÉireann*?" Ned asked.

"Of course. Three of us did. When we were younger."

Ned smirked. "Hope you haven't lost any of your skills with age."

Fionn pointed at Aisling. "Ye have an All-Ireland Button Accordion champion right here. Don't worry about our skills," Fionn said with a forced smile. What a pompous hure this one is, he thought.

"We'll see," Ned said as he gathered the other dancers.

"We've been working on the North Kerry Set. Do you know that music?" Shayla asked Fionn.

"Let's see if I remember, the first four figures are polkas and the fifth is the hornpipe?"

"That's it, Fionn. Well, shall we give it a try?"

Office Mulroney sat in a chair by the far wall sipping coffee from a Styrofoam cup. He was keeping an eye on that Ned, whom he trusted less than Biff the window basher. Shayla was always going on about what a great dancer this Ned guy was. He and Shayla were designated dance partners from the first day she joined the group. That burned Officer Mulroney. He'd never been much of a dancer, and he had to admit he was jealous of how fun this céilí stuff looked. But if the squad caught wind of him tryin' to dance like this, he'd never hear the end of it.

"First figure, North Kerry Set," Ned yelled out to the

dancers. "Now remember this is the star figure. First we all quarterhouse in a complete circle. Then the top couples take their right hands and form a star wheeling clockwise in the center. They switch to their left hands and star counterclockwise back to their places. Finally they swing with their partners in the waltz hold at home. Everyone repeats the quarterhouse. Then the side couples do their stars in the center then swing at home. Then we repeat the entire dance from the top and finish with a quarterhouse. And mind your stars, keep them tight," he said.

Fionn waited for a nod from Ned to start the music, but he wasn't looking his way. Diarmuid shrugged his shoulders and grinned.

"*A haon, a dó, a haon dó trí!*" The band ripped into a fast-paced "Kerry Polka" as the dancers twirled around. Peadar noticed Officer Mulroney's foot was tapping absentmindedly to the music. Hah, we've got him on our side fer sure, he thought. Diarmuid and Fionn were stomping their feet as they played. Aisling closed her eyes and let the music grab hold of all her thoughts, as if every beat of her heart was set to polka time.

The dancers got halfway through the dance when the couple opposite Shayla and Ned made a misstep, became terribly confused and headed the wrong way into the star formation.

"Stop the music!" Ned yelled. He took out his handkerchief and mopped the sweat from his brow, knocking his toupee a bit askew. "I've told you two a million times," he barked at the older couple, "the star is clockwise first. To your *right* first."

"I'm sorry, Ned," the woman said with fear in her eyes. "It's just that the music was so fast."

Ned turned toward the band and said sarcastically, "All-Ireland champion, is that right? I think Officer Mulroney slipped them a fin to make them play so fast they'd kill me."

The policeman, without missing a beat, turned toward Fionn and gave him a thumbs-up sign. Shayla put her hands on her hips and frowned at her husband.

"Remember you're playing for simple country folks here," Ned said to the band. "Keep the speed appropriate."

Diarmuid snickered. "He should see some real culchies dance. They'd have called that there a dirge."

"What's that son?" Ned said leaning toward the band, hand cupped over his ear. "Did I hear someone whining because he can't play willy nilly and has to really work at keeping the tempo danceable?"

Aisling saw Fionn's hand curl into a fist on his lap again. Och, here comes another night of sleeping in a cell, she thought.

"All right everyone. Let's take it from the top." Ned led them back into formation. He turned his head toward Fionn. "Maestro!"

It was a long evening with Ned throwing barbs at both the band and Officer Mulroney every chance he could get. Aisling noticed the fear on the faces of the dancers. They all look petrified that they'd make a mistake incurring the wrath of Ned. Peadar said silent Hail Marys that the dancers would perform each figure correctly so he could finally play a hornpipe for the fifth figure. Fionn's eyes glazed with fatigue. Diarmuid amused himself by picturing Ned dancing in front of a lineup of IRA sharpshooters.

At the end of the fourth figure, the dancers took a water break. Some of the ladies baked soda bread and scones, of which

Office Mulroney had already sampled. Ned saw him eating a scone and smirked.

"Too bad the Irish don't make doughnuts," he said patting his stomach as he sneered at the policeman. "Isn't that your favorite food group?"

Officer Mulroney removed his cap and ran his fingers slowly through his thick head of wavy salt and pepper hair. "I've heard doughnuts boost hair growth," he smiled back at the dance leader whose toupee was now slanting like a jaunty beret.

"Is that so," Ned asked with a sharp laugh. "Then let me see your knuckles, that is, if you can pick them up from dragging on the ground." He laughed as he shoved a piece of soda bread in his mouth and washed it down with tea.

Officer Mulroney knew he'd have to go to confession for the thoughts he was thinking about how to rearrange this dancing prima donna's face. He hated seeing Ned slip his arm around his wife's waist. Hated, hated, *hated* it! What bothered him even more was how relaxed Shayla seemed to be with Ned pawing her like that. Oh, he wished he didn't have two left feet. He wished he could come in there some night with the skills of Michael Flatley and have a dance showdown with this randy geezer who was taking liberties with his wife.

Aisling set down her accordion and wandered over to the refreshments table. She could see the policeman looking forlorn on the side of the room, so she walked over to say hello.

"Are ye a dancer, too?"

"Nah," he said shaking his head. "Too clumsy."

"Aw go on, I bet I could get ye to dance."

Officer Mulroney laughed. "I don't think so."

"Let me show ye the sevens and threes. Learn that and ye can Irish dance." Aisling took his hands and pulled him out of his chair.

"Fionn," she yelled, "give us an easy reel." Ned snickered as he folded his arms to watch. Shayla frowned at the sight of this pretty young Irish girl holding her husband's hands.

"These are basically rock steps," Aisling said as she stood him next to her. "Step back on the left foot, front on the right foot as ye move to the right for seven beats. See that rock-rock movement? Ye've got it. Now, take the right foot and step behind ye, step forward on the left and then back on the right. That's a back, two, three. Now step back with the left, forward with the right, back with the left, that's another back, two three. Then step behind ye with the right, forward on the left as ye count off another seven rock steps going to the left. Then do two more back threes, first stepping back on the left foot." The policeman's face turned beet red as he concentrated on his footwork, which delighted Ned. Officer Mulroney felt very vulnerable as he tried to count aloud and remember which foot went forward and what direction he was heading in.

"Fair play to ye, Officer Mulroney," Fionn yelled. "Look out Mr. Flatley! I think someone wants yer lordship title."

Officer Mulroney laughed, lost the beat and stumbled into Aisling. She patted him on the shoulder. "Yer doin' just fine there." He winked at her. Shayla interrupted.

"We can practice this at home, Jerry."

"But I won't have a live Irish band there," he said to his wife.

One of the other men came over to offer encouragement.

"You're stepping fine there," the man said. "Maybe you'll be joining our céilí dance group soon."

"Don't count on it," Ned sneered. "OK, back to the real dancing. Fifth figure of the North Kerry Set. Hornpipe please, musicians. When you're ready."

"Thank you for the lesson," Officer Mulroney said to Aisling with a big smile on his face.

"It was easy. I think yer a natural." She blew him a kiss as she skipped back over to join the band. Shayla caught the exchange and was furious. Ned noticed her expression and squeezed his arm around her waist as they heel stepped one-two-three toward the center of the group, then stamped their feet back one-two-three to the hornpipe rhythm.

By the time the dancing was over for the evening, Fionn tallied up that they'd been playing about three hours. Had this been a gig, they would have earned a nice paycheck for that. All they earned, though, were no arrests on their personal records, some very dry soda bread and sleep on some unforgiving cots in the jail. He knew things could have been worse, *much* worse and he was grateful for what they had at the moment.

"You kids hungry?" Officer Mulroney asked as they packed their instruments. They looked at each other and nodded.

"There's this diner near the highway. Let me and the wife treat you for the music you gave us this evening. And also for my first dance lesson," he said winking at Aisling. Diarmuid instinctively draped his arm around her as to say, sorry lad, she's taken.

Shayla agreed to his plan but asked if the other dancers could come along, too. All of them declined the invitation except for Ned, of course. He offered to drive Shayla since they all couldn't fit in Officer Mulroney's car.

Dante's Diner was an aluminum Art Deco masterpiece parked on a dead end near the ramp off the interstate. A sign on the door said they were open 'til ten, but since Officer Mulroney was a good friend, the group was welcomed heartily even though it was half an hour before closing.

"Officer Jerry, how are you tonight?" Dante, the owner of the diner said as he wiped his hands on a dish towel and came over to shake hands. "Where'd you find these people?"

"These are my new friends from Ireland. Very talented musicians. I told them what a good cook you are."

Dante looked at the group and recognized Jerry's wife. "Hey Shayla, glad you could stop by tonight." She winked at him, and Aisling giggled as she noticed both Shayla's husband and Ned frown. Officer Mulroney introduced everyone, Ned being last.

"So what's good on the menu tonight?"

Dante scratched his head. "Well, we had a run of truckers this evening so all the specials are gone except I do have some Irish soup, well, it's my corned beef and cabbage soup. But that's not something special for you kids, you probably have that all the time at home. Am I right?"

The musicians drew their mouths into taut grim grins.

"I can make a bunch of grilled cheese sandwiches to go with it, too. How's that sound?"

"Delicious! Thanks Dante," Officer Mulroney said as he

closed up the menu.

"If you have a salad or fruit cup, I'd prefer that instead," Ned said. He looked at Shayla. "I'll have the same, Dante," she added.

"How about you kids?"

"We'll have what he's having," Fionn said pointing at the policeman. Officer Mulroney grinned at them. These were basically good kids. Too bad they got caught up with that bunch of college hooligans last night.

Dante took their drink orders and went back to the griddle. Aisling and Diarmuid saddled up onto the counter stools and amused themselves by spinning around until they were dizzy. Peadar was trying not think how hungry he was and tapped his fingers like he was playing the piano on the counter. Shayla gossiped about the other céilí dancers with Ned. All that the others could hear were wisps and hisses of conversation: "So he goes to me, 'That costume needs some shamrocks to be authentic,' and I go, 'What do you mean? We're wearing something very traditional.' Then he goes, 'Well it sure doesn't look Irish,'" Shayla said, laughing with Ned across the table.

"How do you like America so far?" Officer Mulroney asked Fionn.

"Well, we had a grand time in Boston. Me cousin took us to a Celtics game. We got to play at a pub there. The drive here was beautiful, reminds me quite a bit of back home except ye've got the trees. We were enjoying our workin' holiday. Ever since the car crash, though, we're missin' home a lot."

"Do you have any plans for St. Patrick's Day?"

"Glad ye brought that up, Officer Mulroney."

"Kid, you can call me Jerry."

Fionn smiled. "Fair play to ye, Jerry. So we're goin' to need some money to pay for the car repairs, and we thought maybe we could play somewhere that day. Ye know, a fund raiser for our car."

"Good idea. I admire your work ethic, son."

"Do ye know any place that would be a good venue?"

Dante overheard the conversation as he handed out their drinks.

"My cousin Paulie has a nice restaurant with a big banquet room. He's always letting people hold benefits back there for kids with leukemia, fire victims and stuff like that. I could give him a call and see if he has anything going on in the back room that night."

"That'd be grand, Dante. What's the name of the restaurant?"

"Paulie's Italian Palazzo. They serve lots of 'rigs,' pizza and spaghetti. You know. The usual." Dante shrugged his shoulders and laughed.

Fionn was amused by the thought of a bunch of Irish musicians playing in an Italian restaurant on St. Patrick's Day.

"Can you kids play the tarantella? If so, that'd be a riot. Even I'd pay to see Paulie's eyes pop when you did that. Hah!"

Dante served the band and Officer Mulroney bowls of corned beef and cabbage soup. Shayla and Ned asked for refills of their cups of tea with fresh lemon slices. Like Ned needs any more acid, Officer Mulroney thought as he watched him squeeze every possible drip of juice into his tea.

"I'm going to call Paulie right now," Dante said as he disappeared into the kitchen.

"Ye know, I hate to admit this," Peadar said as slurped his soup, "but I'm starting to develop a likin' fer this stuff."

Aisling grabbed his arm and looked at him with an especially serious expression.

"Resist, Peadar. Don't go over to the dark side."

"That's right lad," Diarmuid said, shaking his head in agreement. "Think of this bowl as sustenance, nothing else. Pinch yer nose if ye have to, then ye won't be associating the smell with a pleasurable taste. Train yer mind to follow the path of truth ... we're not *corned beef eatin' folk*."

"Yez two are daft," Peadar said batting away Aisling's arm. "I'm bleedin' hungry. It tastes feckin' good. Let me ate in peace."

Diarmuid and Aisling laughed.

"Alright, just fer that, yez two, when I get back to Mayo, maybe I'll open up a corned beef take-away."

Fionn winked at Diarmuid and Aisling. "Sounds like ye might need an intervention there, lad. Maybe we could go back to Danu's and have her cast a spell on ye that would make ye impervious to all manner of corned beef." Peadar scrunched up his face at their teasing. They relented when Dante returned with their sandwiches and the salads for Ned and Shayla.

"Hey kids, great news! Paulie's planning a big St. Patrick's Day evening with bagpipers and step dancers. In fact, he already booked another band, but I convinced him to let you kids be the main attraction and that trio be your warm-up act."

Fionn smiled but didn't like the thought of bagpipers, fussy step dancers and some other band joining the bill. It would mean less of a payment for their efforts. Then again, at this point he couldn't afford to be so choosy.

"Thanks a million there Dante for settin' it up for us."

"No problem. I can tell you're good kids."

"Where's the restaurant?" Diarmuid asked.

"Just down the road from Butch's garage, on the outskirts of town."

"That reminds me," Fionn said to Officer Mulroney. "We need to stop by Butch's tomorrow and see if the car is ready. Any chance ye could give us a lift over there?"

Officer Mulroney nodded. "First things first, though. Where are you kids staying tonight?"

Peadar set down his cup of tea. "We're lookin' for suggestions. Some place clean, not expensive and in walking distance. A continental breakfast would be lovely. Any place near Butch's you'd recommend?"

Officer Mulroney sipped his coffee, glanced over at his wife who was chatting animatedly with Ned, and set the mug down on the counter.

"You kids shouldn't have to spend more money over here. Especially after the great concert you gave us for free tonight. I'm sure that Shayla wouldn't mind if you stayed with us for the night, would you honey? We have two spare bedrooms and a couple of couches."

Ned elbowed Shayla. "We should be paying closer attention to their conversation. I just heard your name." Officer Mulroney frowned at him.

"I said you wouldn't mind if these kids stayed with us. Right, honey? We have plenty of food at home and the house is clean—right?"

Ned snickered. "Nice job of backing your wife into a corner. She can't possibly say 'no' in front of them, can she?"

"Of course she can, right Shayla?" Officer Mulroney said as he walked over to her and slid his arm around her waist. "You have the final say in this matter." Ned sneered.

Shayla looked at both men, then the band as she covered her mouth with her hands. She opened her arms grandly toward the band and smiled. "Sure!" she said enthusiastically. "I'd love it! They can stay with us as long as they'd like, that is, if they don't mind playing some music again for us so we can practice our two-hand reel for St. Patrick's Day."

Diarmuid kicked Aisling under the counter. "Incorrigible!" she muttered to him under her breath. She tried to sip her tea, but when Diarmuid kicked her again, she spit some out, laughing.

"We'd love to!" Peadar chirped as he finished chewing the last corner of his grilled sandwich.

"Wonderful! It's a deal then," Shayla said. Fionn's hand curled into a fist on the counter. Aisling noticed how tired he looked and went over to give him a shoulder massage. He smiled at her kind gesture.

"Thanks, luv. I needed that. All this fiddlin' around and goin' nowhere has worn me out."

"You kids look pretty tired," Shayla said. "We should head home so you can all get a good night's sleep."

The Mulroneys had a modest split level home on an acre of land. The first room past the foyer—what would have been used for a dining room in most homes—was more of a game parlor. There were two oversized leather couches, a pool table, dart board, big screen TV and mini-refrigerator. The walls were decorated with Buffalo Bills memorabilia: posters, jerseys, pennants and footballs. Over the fireplace was an autographed photo of former quarterback Jim Kelly, surrounded by cast iron running buffalo bookends.

"Yer a sports fan, I see," Fionn said to Officer Mulroney.

"Yeah, long-sufferin' Bills fan," he sighed. "I follow the Yankees, too, and Syracuse's pro hockey team. How about yourself?"

"Well, I enjoy followin' Clare's Gaelic football team. Me cousin Conor plays for them. He's a brilliant *cúl báire*, ye know, goalkeeper."

"So what's the difference between Gaelic football and American football?" the officer asked as he handed Fionn a beer from the refrigerator.

"Well, it's more like a blend of hurling and rugby."

Officer Mulroney shrugged his shoulders. "Now you're really speaking a foreign language to me. Hah!"

"Well, if you'd like," Fionn said, his eyes twinkling, "we could give ye and the missus a tutorial tomorrow."

"Only if it involves kicking Ned's head," Officer Mulroney whispered with a laugh.

"Consider it done," Fionn said clinking his beer bottle with his.

After Shayla brought out bed linens for Diarmuid and Fionn who'd be sleeping on the couches (Peadar and Aisling accepted the small guest bedrooms), everyone headed to bed. Shayla used a strong lavender-scented fabric softener on the bed linens that relaxed them all into an easy, deep sleep. That is, until the scanner started going off in the middle of the night for a barn fire just on the other side of the hill. The scanner was hooked into the house PA system, so it sounded in every room. They all stirred as they heard Officer Mulroney come out of his bedroom, put on his coat, grab his keys and back the police cruiser out of the driveway. Smoke drifted over the hill and wove its way into their dreams. Peadar dreamed he was running his corned beef take-away on the streets of Westport....

FÁINNE #8

A smoky fog settled over the neighborhood by the time Shayla got up to go to work. Officer Mulroney wasn't back yet from keeping guard at the fire scene. It was a nasty four-alarm blaze and unfortunately some farm animals died. The heat from the leaping flames also melted several telephone wires, cutting the service to the Mulroney home.

Aisling awoke and found a note Shayla left on the kitchen counter that said they could help themselves to whatever food they wanted for breakfast. She'd be back mid-day (she had a part-time job at the county library) and Ned would come over then so they could practice their two-hand reel.

Aisling toasted cinnamon raisin bread she found in a basket and put the kettle on the boil. She peeked in the cupboard and found a collection of fancy cups and saucers designed by Thomas Kinkade, "the painter of light." Shayla also appeared to have a tea hoarding issue, because the next cupboard was filled entirely with boxes of teas—black, green, herbal and fruit flavored. Aisling selected a bag of vanilla chai and whistled "The Cup of Tea" reel as she waited for the kettle to provide some harmony.

"Smells good," Peadar said, sniffing his way into the kitchen. "Any left?"

"Sure, toast it yerself."

"Where is everybody?"

"Dunno." Aisling poured boiling water into the teacup. "From the note Shayla left, guess we have until mid-afternoon to rouse ourselves for her practice with that Ned fella."

"He's an awful hure, ain't he? Poor Officer Mulroney. That Ned's always pawin' his wife in front of him."

"I wouldn't trust Ned with her," Aisling said as she sat down on the leather couch where Diarmuid had slept.

"Defo." Peadar poured some milk in his tea.

The front door opened startling them. "Howya Fionn, Diarmuid? Where yez been?" Peadar asked.

"Shayla gave us a ride to Butch's since Jerry was still out at the fire." Fionn said.

"Well, what's the verdict on the car?" Aisling folded her arms, bracing herself for the answer.

Diarmuid grimaced. "Part's not in yet. Might not be until the end of next week. And the good news is … OK, I lied. The part's gonna cost more than Butch thought."

Aisling gasped. Peadar blessed himself. Each of them stared off in a different direction as they imagined what it would be like to spend another week trapped in this hell.

"I'm gonna see if I can call Des collect on their phone," Fionn said as he picked it up and pushed the zero. He noticed there was no dial tone and clicked the receiver a couple of times. Nothing.

"Would yez feckin' believe our bleedin' luck? *Jaysus*, this is like one of them alien movies."

"Or zombies," Peadar said as he buttered a slice of cinnamon raisin toast and took a bite. Diarmuid rolled his eyes back and started staggering toward Aisling with his arms out.

"Get away from me, ye savage. Cut it out, yer scarin' me. Yer gonna trigger me snake sense." Diarmuid tried to keep a straight face.

"C'mon Aisling, don't ye think he'd makes a dashing zombie?" Fionn teased.

"No! And should I be scared that ye just said that?"

"I am," Peadar laughed.

They ate breakfast, drank several rounds of tea and stared out at the Mulroney's back yard that faced a muddy-bleak field. Crows cawed from the top of an old oak split by a lightning bolt. Every once and a while a car would speed past on the road out front, then the silence would return until the crows flew back to the tree. The four wandered outside through the sliding glass doors with the thought of hanging out on the patio. "Jaysus, it feels hotter than June out," Diarmuid said. They changed plans, returned inside and shot pool for awhile, played darts and then regrouped on the couch, staring back at the cawing crows.

"Ye'd think someone who booked us would have contacted Des by now. Wouldn't he be concerned and have sent someone to rescue us?" Fionn sank his head into his hands and rested his elbows on his knees.

"We could have been eaten by coyotes and no one would know about it." Aisling hugged a throw pillow.

"I wonder if our families even know we're missin,'" Peadar said. "Maybe me Ma went to light some candles at Knock for us."

"What if we can't make our flight back home to Ireland?" Diarmuid asked. He picked at an upholstery button on the couch.

Peadar sighed. Fionn started chewing the fingernail of his right thumb.

"Don't worry, we'll get there soon. Maybe Butch was wrong. Maybe the part will arrive this afternoon and he can finish the car."

They moped about for hours until Peadar unpacked his uilleann pipes and started playing a slip jig. Instinctively, they all wandered over, picked up their instruments, closed their eyes and let the music soothe their fears.

Officer Mulroney arrived home before his wife and gave them a brief wave. He reeked of smoke from the fire and headed straight for the shower after tossing his clothes in the washing machine. Then he crawled into bed for a few hours.

Fionn was concerned that their music might bother him, but knew the poor fella was probably completely knackered from being up so late and wouldn't notice if they didn't play too loudly.

When Shayla returned from work she fixed some sandwiches for a late lunch and called Ned to come over for dance practice. He arrived promptly with some CD music that they always used for their two-hand reel. Fionn wanted to scream when he saw the cover. It was called *Reel Good Aul' Times*—traditional Irish dance music by All-Ireland fiddler Paddy MacSeamus.

"Do you kids think you could play this reel?" Ned said as he played the track "Pigeon on the Gate." Fionn's hands rolled into fists as he heard Paddy saw his nearly tuned fiddle while he lilted "Diddle diddle eye o, diddle diddle eye o, diddle dee diddle dee diddle diddle eye o."

Ned smirked at Fionn's reaction. "Of course this fella is a professional, so I expect his quality of playing to be a bit beyond you traveling musicians."

What the feck? Fionn thought as he lifted his fists to his chin. What's this feckin' eejit tellin' us? How'd he like it if we criticized his dancin' like a feis adjudicator? Bet he'd run cryin' back home to his mam, Fionn thought. Aisling reached over and rubbed his back again and Fionn relaxed his hands. Diarmuid was uncomfortable with Fionn's growing dependance on Aisling's soothing touch, but he knew it was better than watching Fionn unleash his pent-up Paddy rage.

Fionn nodded at Peadar, picked up his fiddle and counted off as the two started playing "Pigeon On The Gate." Shayla clapped her hands together.

"You sound just like the CD! Only you're live."

Only we're in tune, Fionn thought as he gritted his teeth and stared at Ned waiting for his reaction to their music. Ned sneered and took Shayla's hands to get into position for the start of the dance, then he released one and made a "slow down" gesture to the band. Diarmuid strummed a tad slower and the other musicians caught the beat he was setting. Ned and Shayla danced off to the center of the room, he turned her under his arms a couple of times, then they crossed arms in front of themselves and danced to the right, then back to the center, then off to the left for the same number of counts. Fionn noted Ned's stern expression. With that silly toupee and poor excuse for a mustache, he could have been goose-stepping to a military band. Shayla, on the other hand, had rosy cheeks and smiled so wide her dimples were like caverns. She had a light step that betrayed her girth and Fionn felt she looked more like one of the dancers he'd seen back home at a kitchen céilí.

The two dancers dropped hands and took turns doing their solos. Ned danced forward, grim-faced, rocked a few sean-nós steps then danced back next to Shayla. She danced forward, kicked her legs up lively with some flourishes before returning next to Ned.

"Whom are you trying to impress?" Ned said as they took hands and paraded around the room.

"Impress? I was just having some fun. Their music inspires me," Shayla said as Ned spun her around a couple of times again.

"Just thought you were trying to be *Michaela* Flatley," Ned said with heavy humor. Shayla knew that meant she was dancing better than he was and he didn't like the thought of attention being drawn away from him.

Officer Mulroney awoke from his nap and shuffled into the kitchen, fixed a bowl of raisin bran and sat on the couch to watch. The smoke from last night's fire still clung to him, annoying Ned. He grinned as he shoveled a tablespoon of cereal into his mouth.

When the two-hand reel was done, Officer Mulroney set down his empty bowl and turned toward the band.

"You kids psyched for St. Patrick's Day tomorrow?"

"As psyched as we can be, I suppose," Peadar said.

"Well, don't know how you celebrate in Ireland," the officer said, "but over here, people get a bit crazy."

"I've heard this time referred to as the 'high holy days,' although there seems nuthin' too holy about 'em," Peadar said. "What can ye expect though, celebrating Ireland's most famous saint?"

"He wasn't Irish, you know," Ned said smugly, arms folded.

"Of *course* he was!" Shayla said, rolling her eyes

apologetically toward the band.

"Actually not. Historians say he was from what the area known as Wales today."

"St. Patrick was Welsh?" Shayla frowned. "Is that true?" she asked the band with the face of a child who's just learned Santa's awful truth.

"No one knows fer sure," Fionn said. "One thing is probably certain, he had Celtic heritage. We're all Celts. What's the bloody difference?"

"I think I just heard a historian groan somewhere," Ned said. "Now, can we give the North Kerry Set a try again?"

"Can't really call it a set, can ye there Ned? Ye know, with only one couple." Diarmuid said as he tuned the D string on his guitar, grinning toward Aisling.

"Set refers to a group of dances with similar themes, not a specific number of dancers." Ned snapped back.

"That'd be news to the Irish Dance Commission," Aisling said with a straight face. The band snickered.

"Honey, do we still have to go to that Lady Friends of Erin thing tonight?" Officer Mulroney whined as he sipped coffee.

"Oh, dear!" Shayla said clasping her hands to her face. "I nearly forgot. I have to bake some soda bread for that."

"I'm so tired from last night. I don't think I have the strength, hon," Officer Mulroney said as he stretched out on the couch. "This is supposed to be my weekend, after all, and you know they'll be calling me tomorrow when the craziness starts."

"Jerry! You promised to help with the history presentation. You *have* to be there. I don't know how to run that computer slide show thingy."

Ned twitched with impatience at their squabbling on his valuable time. "Are we here to dance or socialize?"

Diarmuid snickered. Ned glared. Diarmuid stuck out his tongue.

"Wouldn't the Irish Dance Commission like to see that type of behavior from so-called professional musicians? Come on, back to the North Kerry."

"Oh! I just thought of something. We should bring the band along tonight. You kids could have a free meal in exchange for playing for our St. Patrick's Eve sing-along. Wouldn't that be fun?"

Officer Mulroney carried his dishes into the kitchen and as he passed by the musicians, whispered, "About as much fun as dental surgery."

The Lady Friends of Erin, Division Six, met in a hall in the basement of the fire station. When the Mulroneys walked in with the band, the ladies twittered with excitement that they were in the presence of genuine Irish people. The smallish room was crowded with cafeteria-sized tables covered with green linen tablecloths, battery-powered twinkling tea lights and small Irish crystal vases filled with green-tipped carnations.

"Let me introduce you to our president, Kitty MacNamara," Shayla said as she handed her soda bread to another member, took Fionn's hand and crossed the room.

"Division Six? Ye have that many Irish-American ladies out here?"

"Oh, no, there's only been one *official* group here since it started. From time to time there have been a few splits in the organization. This one didn't like what that one said or did. Someone trampled over parliamentary procedure. That sort of thing. You get the picture. But like a creek hitting a few boulders, the split divisions always eventually flowed back into one organization."

"How old is yer group?"

"We've been together almost seven years now. Isn't that wonderful?"

Fionn smirked as they approached the current president. Kitty was on the negative side of five feet tall and wore a broad green suit with a carnation stuck in her lapel that matched the ones on the tables. Her hair was pulled back with a green velvet headband that framed her high, square forehead and equally square jaw. Her thick eyebrows knit together like clasped hands as she listened to Shayla make introductions and let Fionn explain what type of music they could play for the ladies.

Kitty put her hands on her wide hips and looked around the room.

"I wish you had called me about this, Shayla. We could have set up a place for them to play."

"Sorry, Kitty, but our phone is out from the fire up on Hard Knock Hill last night. Burned the wires."

Kitty looked at the musicians' unkempt clothes. This wasn't proper attire for one of their elegant evenings. Shayla was so enthusiastic about these kids, though. Perhaps if they were tucked in the far corner, they wouldn't distract from the perfectly set atmosphere.

"All right then. They can play over there by St. Florian. We'll let them get in the buffet line once all of the ladies have gotten their meals."

The band set up their equipment under the plaster statue of the patron saint of firefighters. Aisling's chair had to be propped up in the midst of a display of fire extinguishers due to the constricted space. It was stifling hot in the room. (Although there had been a record high temperature in the seventies that afternoon, heat was pouring out of the old radiators behind them.) The four fanned themselves as they waited patiently for the ladies to go through the buffet line. Peadar worried that there'd be none left for them by the time he got up there, and his stomach rumbled in protest.

When the women were seated, Kitty nodded at the band members to come up and fill their plates. Peadar was first in line and was happy to see that there was enough left for all of them to eat. Problem was, he had no idea what the breaded log-shaped food in the first warming tray was or the pinkish sauce next to it. He asked Kitty. She was not impressed by his lack of culinary *savoire-faire*.

"They're croquettes. Corned beef croquettes. This is the Russian dressing you dip them in."

Aisling's stomach rolled over and played dead and the mention of the CB words again. *Och, what I'd give for good chipper take-away,* she thought.

Shayla signaled to her husband (who was playing solitaire on the kitchen counter as he waited) that it was time to get the evening's video presentation ready. He rolled the TV cart into the hall, plugged in the equipment and inserted a disc into the DVD player.

It was a tradition to share some Irish history via an audio-visual presentation at every Lady Friends of Erin gathering. Tonight's video was about the Great Irish Famine. The ladies shook their heads as their forks slid into green ambrosia salad, scooped up garlic mashed potatoes and dipped corned beef croquettes into the dressing.

"Look at those poor children," Kitty said as she wiped mashed potatoes from the corner of her mouth with her napkin. "Lifeless, clinging to their parents. Hard to believe the cruelty mankind is capable of," she said as she buttered a slab of soda bread.

Fionn recognized that photo from the national archives. It showed a starving family in Carraroe, Connemara, huddled lifelessly in their empty cottage. He looked around the room and realized that probably most of these women had ancestors who fled to America because of the darkest moment in Irish history. What made him angry was the fact that there *was* food during the famine, but the British shipped it out of Ireland. There was no need for any of these people to starve to death, nearly a million by some counts. And many more fled Ireland, Fionn thought. Here were their descendants in America, trying to grasp onto bits of history and culture of their ancestral homeland that for some was little more than a genetic memory.

"We have a special treat this evening," Kitty said standing up as the green-iced cupcakes topped with plastic shamrocks were delivered to the tables. "For our sing-along, we will be accompanied by these musicians direct from Ireland." The women turned toward the band and applauded.

"Ladies, take out your sing-along books. Let's start with 'If You're Irish, Come Into the Parlour.' Bandleader, if you would be so kind to give us our starting note."

Fionn looked at the others. "Anyone know this song? I have no idea what feckin' key it's in. Suggestions?"

"Start in D," Diarmuid said. "When in doubt, give them D."

Fionn played a D note on his fiddle and Kitty started singing the song as the band took a couple of bars to catch the melody and follow. He thought they did pretty well for not knowing the melody at all.

"Well done, ladies!" Kitty beamed when they finished. "Now, turn to page 6 for 'My Wild Irish Rose.'"

Aisling caught Diarmuid smirking at her and looked down at the keyboard on her accordion. When she looked up, he was still grinning at her. She hit a wrong note, and Kitty glared at them. Aisling smiled and got back into the melody, trying to ignore Diarmuid although she could still see his devilish grin out of the corner of her eye. She was happy when the song ended, and mouthed to Diarmuid, "Stop it!"

"Who would like to suggest the next song?" Kitty said looking around the room.

Diarmuid whispered, "Why don't yez sing 'Far, Far Away.'" Aisling giggled, she couldn't help herself. All the ladies turned and tsk-tsked the pair for their rudeness. Fionn stood up and spoke, hoping to distract the attention away from his bandmates.

"Do yez know 'My Lovely Rose of Clare'?" he asked, thinking the song would fit the genre of schmaltzy songs they were singing. "It's a lovely song, popular back home."

"It's not in the book," Kitty lowered her eyebrows and the ragtag musicians and frowned. "Now then, who's got another suggestion?"

"Watch it, yez two," Fionn whispered to Diarmuid and Aisling. "We can't be embarrassing Shayla and Jerry."

"Good suggestion, Martha," Kitty said. "'Mother Machree,' it is. Ready, ladies?"

Fionn and the band played their restrained accompaniment for an hour or so. It was uninspired and laborious and frankly, it was hell. No chance to liven the pace. No chance to show off their skills. They couldn't wait to get back to the Mulroneys' home and go to bed. Tomorrow would be a long day, they could all sense it. Officer Mulroney was still tired from the night before, so he was happy to see them all eager to turn in early.

A few hours later, silence in the pitch-black house was shattered when the scanner went off again in the middle of the night. Fionn awoke and was confused for a few minutes. Where was he? Why couldn't he see anything? Had he gone blind? As he drifted back to sleep, he heard a dispatcher saying something about a van sliding into the ditch on State Route 392. Diarmuid woke up just then, too, and drifted off to sleep as the dispatcher said that the driver saw a black pony run in front of the vehicle, startling him and causing him to swerve off the road.

The scanner conversation wove into Aisling's dream, and she interpreted it as a report that a giant corned beef was chasing a Connemara pony down the road when they were hit by a conga line of drunk céilí dancers led by Paddy MacSeamus up the hill. A coyote howling outside the Mulroney home woke her and she sat up, blanket drawn to her neck as she tried to see in the dark room if a coyote was circling her bed. For a second, she thought she saw a pair of red glowing eyes and screamed. The púca! Aisling's teeth chattered. She tugged the covers over her head, lay back down and curled into a fetal position on the bed.

Peadar's rhythmic snoring was broken by Aisling's scream. He snuffled, sat up and looked around, then his head fell back onto the pillow and he started dreaming about driving his corned beef croquettes take-away van down the streets of Westport, Mayo.

Officer Mulroney was usually a light sleeper and the mere crackle of the scanner would rouse him. Not this night. Neither the sirens in the background nor the conversation between his partner racing to the accident scene and the dispatcher directing him were enough to wake the policeman up.

The scanner quieted down and all within the Mulroney household were fast asleep again.

FÁINNE #9

Ned knocked on the Mulroney's door just after noon. When no one answered, he peeked in their garage and saw the car was there. He pounded on the door, figuring maybe Shayla had the dishwasher or clothes dryer running and couldn't hear him. The bright sun heated his back like a skillet on a camp fire and he took off his leather jacket, folded it neatly over his arm and banged on the door with his other hand.

This wasn't like Shayla. She was always prompt, oftentimes early to their performances. Their dance group had been asked to perform at the senior center's St. Patrick's Day party this afternoon. Ned suggested that they meet there early so he could set up the CD player and they could have a brief run through of their show.

He knocked once more and yelled out "SHAYLA!" The door swung open and Peadar, wearing a fuzzy pink bathrobe, squinted into the sunlight. He waved Ned inside where all of them were sitting around the kitchen table wearing ill-fitting clothes, looking very tired.

"Did you all go on a bender last night? What's the matter with you?"

"Have a seat, Ned." Shayla said as she went off to grab her costume that was hanging in the bedroom closet, neatly ironed. When they went home last night, she'd stayed up very late to do some laundry, including the band members' clothes. She went through the closets and found some old clothes for the group to sleep in while their clothes were washed.

"That's OK, I prefer to stand," he said keeping a safe distance from the very pink Peadar.

"See you all at Paulie's tonight. Break a leg, kids," Shayla said as she bent down to give her husband a kiss.

"Meet you there, honey," Officer Mulroney said to her. "And no speeding up 392," he said wagging his finger toward Ned. "There was a bad accident up there again last night."

Aisling's eyes grew wide when she remembered her frightening dream.

"What's the matter with ye?" Diarmuid said, noticing her face had grown pale suddenly.

"I had an awful dream last night. That Connemara pony we almost hit was being chased by a giant corned beef." Peadar, Fionn and Diarmuid snickered. "And then, they ran into Paddy MacSeamus leading a 'Sweets of Mayhem' conga line up the road."

"Yer right, lass. It *was* a nightmare," Fionn laughed as he sipped his tea. "So what time does yer man want us to arrive at his restaurant?" Fionn asked Officer Mulroney.

"Paulie said you're supposed to go on at eight, but the parking around there is horrible. On a busy day like today, we should get you there by five at the latest."

"Three hours early?"

Officer Mulroney nodded. "Trust me. Cars will be double parked on that narrow street, making the traffic slow down. Maybe four would be wiser."

Fionn looked at the clock and saw that this meant they'd be leaving in a few hours. "Why don't yez take turns in the shower and we'll have a quick run through the set list after that?"

Thankfully, they took Officer Mulroney's advice and left early. The street was choked with revelers who'd walked in from the hillside or hitched rides on the college shuttle buses to celebrate. Paulie's Italian Palazzo was a standalone white stucco building with faux marble columns supporting a black canopy entrance. Several people stood outside smoking and laughing. Shimmery clover balloons tethered to the flagpole bobbed in the breeze below the green, white and red of Italy.

Peadar hissed. "Och, the eejits! They're supposed to be shamrocks. Do ye not know Patrick used its three leaves on one stalk to explain the concept of the Holy Trinity to the pagans? Ye've got a bunch of four-leafed clovers there. Does any American even know who St. Patrick was?"

"Peadar?" Aisling said, tapping his arm.

"Yes, luv?"

"Who are ye talkin' to?"

"Meself, obviously." He pouted and shook his head toward the window.

"I'll let you kids off here and find some place legal to park," Officer Mulroney said with a hearty laugh.

The band entered the small foyer of Paulie's restaurant where a fountain of a cherub tilting a pitcher gurgled in front of a flocked velvet wall. There were two signs—one pointed to the left toward the bar and bistro area, one pointed to the right toward the banquet hall. That's where they'd be playing.

A waiter brushed past them to the right carrying two pitchers of green beer.

"Well, might as follow him in and check out the space where we're playing," Fionn said. A hand-lettered poster had been set up on an easel outside the banquet room. "Welcome to the St. Patrick's Day Festa featuring the world's longest all-you-can-eat corned beef and cabbage buffet for just $9.99/person! (Under age five eat free!) Entertainment by the McCool School of Irish Dance, the Kennedy Céilí Dancers and Leppo the Irish Clown. Music by The Sham Rockers featuring 'The Irish Elvis' with special musical guests from Ireland!"

"Why is that written as guests, plural?" Fionn asked.

"Look around, boyo, I count four of us. We're plural." Diarmuid replied.

"Come on, lad," Peadar said. "How many other Irish musicians do ye think have gotten lost around here the last week."

"Yer right. Don't mind me. Still tired from me restless sleep."

Aisling remembered her dream from the night before and shuddered. She planned to stay as far away from the corned beef buffet as possible.

A woman sitting at a linen-draped card table inside the banquet room greeted them. "Hi, do you have reservations for tonight?" she asked, tapping a list of names with a pencil.

"We're the entertainment," Fionn said.

"Oh, are you the Irish Elvis? I can't wait to hear you sing."

Fionn tilted his head toward the others and whispered, "Jayz, been here so long I look like feckin' Elvis now?" They sniggered and he turned back to the woman. "No, luv, we're the special guests from Ireland on that poster."

"Oh." She looked disappointed.

"Where are we supposed to set up?" Diarmuid asked.

"That's the stage, over there."

The band looked at what was less a stage than a bit of a rise in the floor. In front of the space, workers were arranging and setting tables. Two burly men hoisted large speakers onto poles and plugged them into the sound system. They set up several microphones around the space.

"Howya," Fionn said as he walked over to greet them. "We're the band from Ireland, the main act fer tonight."

"I thought there were two bands," the young man said, not looking up.

"Well, yes, there's the opening act and us."

"I mean two bands from Ireland."

"Oh, ye mean the poster, the way it's phrased? We thought the same thing. As far as we know it's just us."

"Whatever you say, bud. The dinner starts here at 5:30. You might want to get a drink at the bar. You've got a few hours before you go on."

"Sounds like a good idea. Can ye keep an eye on our instruments if we leave them over there."

"Sure."

The band wandered over to the bar side of the building. They could barely wedge their way into the place. Over the shouts of revelers, the Clancy Brothers were waking Finnegan from the dead via jukebox. A group of drunk college girls wearing flashing shamrock-shaped sunglasses watched the band from the bar. One girl approached them and poked Diarmuid in the chest.

"Hey, where's your green beer?"

"Never drank it, never will!" he snapped at her.

"You're no fun. What about you?" she asked as she poked Peadar.

"I don't drink much, luv. But I'd love a mineral water." He smiled at the girl who looked at him as if he'd just said he drank scorpion juice.

"He's lyin' to yez," Aisling said with a smirk. "Loves to drink flaming shots."

"I do not! That there's a lie!"

"He does, and afterward ... let's just say girls that all the ladies *love* him!"

Peadar blushed as the girls with the flashing sunglasses surrounded him.

"Let's get him a green beer!" one yelled. A girl with a green felt-tip marker drew a four-leafed clover on Peadar's face. Another one took a can of sparkly green spray-on hair color and covered his curly locks with it. Then one wearing fake leprechaun ears handed him an Irish car bomb and demanded that he drink it as a shot, not sip it.

By the time Peadar was handed back to the band, Fionn barely recognized him. His face had green lipstick kisses plastered all over it.

"Jayz, what the feck happened to ye?" Fionn shook his head and stared at the vivid sight before him.

"Are ye tryin' to steal Leppo the Clown's job, Peadar?"

Diarmuid said as he scratched his goatee.

"Love the new hair color, *very* posh." Aisling winked as she ruffled his bangs.

"Och, me Da would go bleedin' mental if he saw me now," Peadar said as he saw his reflection in a Genny Cream Ale mirror.

"What time is it, Fionn? Think we should go back to the other room and check on our instruments?" Diarmuid asked.

"Yez can stay here. I'll go have a gander."

When Fionn returned to the banquet room, he was surprised to see many of the tables filled up already. Entire families were sitting at tables, the adults swilling green beer as the young children roamed the dance floor where Leppo the Clown was handing out plastic bags of Lucky Charms cereal. Great, Fionn thought, sugar up the kids while the parents mellow out. Guess who'll be their babysitters?

"It looks like the show will be starting soon," Fionn said when he caught up with the band again in the bar. "We should probably get back over there. I hope ye don't frighten the customers away, boyo," he said as he shook Peadar's shoulders. By the time they entered the banquet room, it was as crowded as the bar. They could see an empty table back to the right of the stage, moved their instruments by it and claimed the table as their own.

The lights dimmed and a spotlight shone toward the entrance. Drone-ful bleating clued them that a pipe band was about to invade the room. The Keltic Kilters strode in proudly to the beat of the snare drum, their pipes screech-bleating up to the opening note of "Scotland the Brave." Paulie's Palazzo was not designed with great acoustics in mind, just enough space to feed as many people as possible in one sitting. That meant a wall of sound at earsplitting volume shadowed the pipe band as it moved around the room.

"God help us," Aisling said, plugging her ears.

"I bet they go into 'The Minstrel Boy,' followed by 'Amazing Grace' and finish with a reprise of "Scotland the Brave," Fionn whispered to Diarmuid. He nodded. "They might throw in a bit of 'Rising of the Moon,' too." Diarmuid whispered. "I think yer right, forgot that one. They're not bad—too bad the acoustics are."

When the pipe band finally snare-drummed out of the room, Paulie took the microphone.

"Top o' the evenin' to ye!" he bellowed. "I'm Paulie O'Formaggio. Welcome to my O'Palazzo! Help yourself to the o'buffet and pitchers of o'green beer. Now, give a palazzo-sized welcome to The Sham Rockers, featuring their very special guest."

Three middle-aged men took the stage. They wore a gaudy combination of lime-green polyester shirts with matching pants, orange cummerbunds and white bow ties. One sat behind a small drum set, the others played bass and lead guitar. They began with a Beatles-esque version of "The Irish Washerwoman" and the crowd erupted into a manic jig-for-all. The commotion drew onlookers from the bar, most weren't allowed in because they didn't have reservations. Peadar saw the college girls who'd absconded with him hovering by the entrance and he broke into a cold sweat. What'll they do to me if they get a hold of me again, he wondered.

Once the crowd was primed, the lead guitarist took the microphone.

"Ladies and gentlemen, direct from Loughlin, Nevada, we present tonight for your listening pleasure …," the drummer rolled his sticks over the snare, "*The Irish Elvis!*" Cymbals crashed! Men at a nearby table hooted and hollered, and those girls from the bar wolf-whistled. A fire-bright spotlight followed a man with a flame red Elvis hairdo and lime-green sparkly cape as he wove his way through the crowd.

"Thank ye, thank ye very much," he said as he grabbed the mic and counted off to the band, "one, two, one two three four!" Fionn put his head in his hands as the Irish Elvis started singing about not stepping on his green suede shoes. The rest of the bandmembers tried in vain to stifle their laughter. That first song morphed quickly into "Return to Bender," "All Fooked Up," and of course, the Irish Elvis classic, "Can't Help Falling In Pubs."

The Irish Elvis combined the essence of his namesake with the added swagger of Michael Flatley as he busted some faux *Riverdance* moves. All of the women in the room—except of course, Aisling—were mesmerized by his tight pleather pants and hairy chest. She was laughing so hard that she feared her spleen would burst.

It wasn't lost on Fionn that the crowd was responding really, *really* well to these sham rockers. They'd be a tough act to follow, he thought, especially after they brought the house down with the closing song of their first set, "Viva, Potatoes!"

Diarmuid turned his head and noticed the room was suddenly overrun with people lining the back wall. Had the restaurant overbooked? He got his answer soon enough when the first glint of tiaras caught his eye. Oh *jayz*, it's the step dancer entourage.

"How 'bout that Irish Elvis?" Paulie said when he grabbed

the mic. "We've got a real o'treat for you now, folks—the award-winning McCool School of Irish Dance." Mr. McCool walked out with a CD player that he plugged into the wall and queued up a tune.

"Good evening. I'm Kevin McCool and tonight the girls will show you some of the dances they are preparing for the upcoming feis season. Starting off, the Murphy sisters will dance the three-hand reel."

Fionn and the others looked around the room nervously to see if Brian and Kelli Murphy were anywhere near. "There they are," Fionn whispered. "Standing by the entrance. Ye don't suppose they've seen us?"

Aisling looked over at the dancers who frowned back at her. "No, but the little she devils have."

The crowd clapped enthusiastically as Katie, Kara and Keera danced the three-hand reel to a recording by Paddy MacSeamus. Fionn gritted his teeth every time he heard Paddy bow the out-of-tune fiddle.

"*Jayz*, that's feckin' brutal to listen to." He pushed clenched fists against his ears.

"Ye know what ye need," Peadar said. "One of them Irish car bombs. That'd set ye right."

"Hah! Ye make a good point there, lad."

Next a large group of dancers got up and formed three circles of six to dance the Fairy Reel. On this recording, Paddy switched from his out of tune fiddle to a shrill tin whistle. Fionn could stand it no more. He walked over to the girls they'd met in the bar, draped his arms around them and told them he needed an Irish car bomb. NOW! They dragged him off gleefully, and when he returned, his hair color matched Peadar's and he was sporting a fake shamrock tattoo on his face. Fionn was so emboldened by the crazy concoction he drank that he walked past Brian and Kelli deliberately and said hello. Diarmuid and Aisling cringed as they watched the interchange.

"We're never gonna get out of this place alive," Diarmuid said.

After the dancers finished their show, half of the customers got up and left. Irish Elvis wasn't too happy to see it, either, when he returned from his break. He gestured at the band to crank up their playing speed as he started singing, "A Little Less Intoxication," then did a quick segue into "Heartbeer Hotel."

Leppo the Irish Clown honked his way through the banquet room and stopped every few tables to make balloon shamrocks for the children. He was a queer-looking squat fellow, with plastic clip-on Vulcan ears, a shiny fake orange beard and a tall green felt hat. A black pipe, with no tobacco in it, dangled from his mouth as he focused intently on twisting the balloons just so. The problem was, the pipe had some rough edges (being carved from a piece of blackthorn stick) and Leppo ended up popping loudly more balloons than the Irish Elvis could take. He stopped the band suddenly while singing "Hound Póg" (no one knew enough to tell him that the Irish word for kiss was pronounced with a long O, but Diarmuid gave him props for attempting to sing in Irish). His upper lip quivered as he sneered at Leppo.

"Hey, clown! You wanna pipe down over there? We're trying to sing here and it's a little hard to do when you're popping them balloons. Look at the crowd. They're all shook up! Uh-huh huh. Find a new place to dwell, will yah?"

Leppo took a bag of multicolored candy out of his pocket, ripped it open with his teeth and then tossed its contents at Irish Elvis. "Hey, Mr. O'Pelvis! Taste the fookin' rainbow!"

Irish Elvis started to run after the insolent leprechaun but skittered over the shiny candies underfoot and fell to the floor.

"Come here, you little squirt!" Irish Elvis yelled as he got back on his feet and chased him through the crowd.

The doorway vanished behind an incoming swarm of women wearing frilly white blouses, green wool skirts and sashes saying Lady Friends of Erin, Division #6. Kitty MacNamara was on lead kazoo as they marched in following her singing "It's a Great Day for the Irish." Their close-knit formation was too tight for Leppo or Irish Elvis to break through, so the pair chased each other around the corned beef dinner buffet as the women started the crowd singing "When Irish Eyes Are Smiling." Every once in a while, one of the ladies would have to duck to avoid being hit by a potato or hunk of cabbage flung by Leppo to keep Irish Elvis at bay.

Paulie walked in from the bar and was horrified to see the hijinks of the two entertainers. He whistled two short notes and a big fella wearing a wife beater with an apron over it—yet still displaying well-hewn biceps—marched over, grabbed the two by the scruffs of their necks and dumped them on the sidewalk out front, the Lady Friends of Erin singing "MacNamara's Band" in formation as they followed behind.

"I don't ever wanna see you bums in here again," he said.

Irish Elvis pulled his cape over his head in shame so no one would recognize him tossed out to the curb. Leppo laughed and made a balloon crown that he set on his head. Irish Elvis was incensed. He popped the balloon crown, stood up and sneered off into the sunset.

"Hey, kids, you're on!" Paulie said pointing at Fionn and the band. Peadar looked at his watch.

"But it's an hour early."

"Don't worry, I've got more entertainment coming. I want to keep these people happy. Don't even think of pulling any crap like those two, either. *Capisce?*"

The band set up quickly in the space vacated by Irish Elvis's group. People were talking so loudly, they could barely hear each other as they tuned up their instruments. This frustrated Fionn, but he also realized that at this noise level, no one would notice that they weren't exactly in tune.

"OK, we'll have to keep this lively," Fionn said to the rest as they waited for their introduction.

Paulie grabbed the mic. "Are we having O'Fun yet?" Whoops rose from the audience. "I just wanted to remind those in the buffet line that we have plenty more rigatonis coming, so if you didn't get any yet, come back in a few minutes. OK, today we have some real musicians from Ireland. First up is a band called True West. Let's give them a hand."

Peadar, Diarmuid and Aisling gave Fionn a puzzled look.

"Sorry, guess the name got lost in translation." He winked at them and they tossed their heads back in laughter. Fionn noted briefly that Paulie said "first up," but then shifted his focus to the task at hand. Nothing could prepare them now for what should prove to be their toughest gig in America yet.

"A haon, a dó, a haon dó trí...." Fionn fiddled light and lively "Banish Misfortune," and immediately every child in the place ran up to the dance floor and began swirling around like fairies, running in circles and doing Isadora Duncan-style interpretations of the jig. The room was electric, and the band felt it literally bouncing with the energy from all the revelers. As soon as the jig was done, they started some reels, "The Ash Plant," then "Drowsy Maggie," and then switched to an even faster jig with "The Mist on the Mountain." The children dancing in front of them sensed the difference in tempo and started running in a circle counterclockwise. Then an older man wearing a Notre Dame sweatshirt, pint of Guinness hat and waggin' a shillelagh danced into the center of their circle, stuck his hands on his hips and danced a spastic jig that forced Peadar to look away because he was so off the beat. He wasn't the only one distracted. Aisling stared at the children circling and circling the dance floor, their movement drawing her eyes round and round like a pen stuck in a Spirograph.

Fionn sensed at the end of the jig that the band needed a breather from the fast pace. After the applause, he stopped to give the names of the tunes and introduce the band members. Just then an ample woman wearing a gold lamé jacket and a wreath of shiny shamrocks in her short, curly hair whispered to Diarmuid that she'd like to sing "Danny Boy" next. Diarmuid took one look at her and couldn't imagine any accurate musical notes coming from her. Oh jayz, he knew he'd have to lie to her.

"Sorry, luv. The owner told us to play lively music only."

"The owner's my uncle!" she glowered and folded her arms,

tapping her foot as she waited for Diarmuid to get Fionn's attention about the addition to their playlist. Diarmuid made sure to mention this woman's genetic connection to the owner. Fionn saw the fear in his eyes and decided not to fight it.

"And now, we've got a very special treat for yez," Fionn said as he leaned toward the woman. "What's yer name, luv?" he whispered.

"Concetta Tagliatelle."

"Right then, folks, the lovely Concetta will sing us a song I think ye'll recognize." Everyone paused as the spotlight bounced around the room off her shiny jacket.

"What key would ye like there, luv?" Diarmuid asked.

"I'll start, and then you follow. I don't know the key."

Oh shite, Diarmuid thought. No good could come from this.

"Ohhhh, Danny Boy...," Concetta started. What blasted key was she in, Diarmuid thought as he tried out several chords on the guitar. Not D, that would be easy. Nor G, nor F, nor C, nor even feckin' A! Bet this beast is singing sharps or flats, he thought. Sure enough, she was singing the song in the key of G flat. This had to be a first!

Fionn was shrugging his shoulders at Diarmuid looking for a clue.

"It's feckin' G flat!"

"Are ye kiddin' me? No one feckin'...."

"I know, Fionn. One for the Guinness Book."

Aisling and Peadar decided wisely to sit this one out. They cringed as Concetta, whose eyes were closed as she clasped her hands to her bosom dramatically, told the sad tale of that Danny lad, struggling with each note to retain any sense of tempo or, by that count, melody. When he wasn't squinting from the aural agony, Fionn looked out at the audience rapt with attention at Concetta's plaintive performance. He could tell they would be begging for an encore. Shite and onions, was there no way out of this hell?

People wept when she finished, and not for the same reason that tears were streaming down Aisling and Peadar's faces.

"Brava! Brava!" Paulie shouted from the back of the banquet room as he ran up with a bouquet of roses to hand his niece. He kissed her and the crowd roared.

"I think my niece deserves an encore, don't you kids?" Paulie said, turning to the band. They nodded with gritted teeth.

"Do you know that song about the unicorn?" Concetta asked.

Fionn closed his eyes for a moment, giving her the impression that he was trying to remember the melody or the words. What he was actually doing was a creative visualization. In it he was standing on the edge of the Cliffs of Moher, screaming, "Feckin' bloody hell, I feckin' hate this shite, I'm gonna feckin' leap right now like them fairy foals and end it all so I won't have to listen to another torturous note from this feckin' COW! You win, Renny! You feckin' WIN! I'll never be famous. There, can we go back home to Ireland now?"

Fionn turned to her, opened his eyes and smiled, "Of course, luv. Shall we start it or follow ye?"

"That sounded great just now. Let me start again."

"As ye wish," Fionn said bowing to her demand.

When the children heard she was going to sing that song about Noah's ark and the unicorns that didn't make it on the boat before the Great Flood, they jumped up and down with excitement.

"I'll show them how to do the hand movements, too," Concetta said. Fionn nodded. As Concetta started singing "The Unicorn Song," Diarmuid tilted his head so he could discern better what key she was singing in this time. It took him until almost the chorus before he shouted to Fionn, "F sharp!"

When Concetta reached the familiar chorus, a group of college kids from the bar burst through the entrance, ignoring the reservation lady, and ran up to the dance floor with their pints in hand. Their bobbing shamrock headbands sometimes moved in tandem, sometimes went their own direction. The kids were a bit unsteady, so they bunched up to stay vertical on the dance floor.

Concetta brought her arms together in front of her to make the gesture of the snapping green alligator's jaw, curved her arms to show long-necked geese, made triangles on her shoulders for humpty-back camels then danced around like a chimpanzee, scratching her side. For cats and rats she mimed whiskers coming from her face (though she really didn't need to mime that) and then she stretched out her arm long, curling her hand at the end, like an elephant's trunk. She spun around at the chorus's end, miming a unicorn horn coming out of her forehead.

The children did look cute, Fionn had to admit, as they followed Concetta's unicorn theater. As for the college kids, that was another story. They slurred their words and gestures as foam from their Guinnesses slid airborne and landed like white skullcaps on the heads of the children. Peadar was worried that they were getting the dance floor so wet that somebody was going to slip, fall and break a bone or poke their eyes out. He had quite the active imagination, that one.

Mercifully, the song had just six verses, unlike some of the epic *sean-nós* songs back home, Fionn thought. Concetta took her bows as the audience leapt to its feet. How the feck could they follow that? He asked the band what they should play next. They discussed this reel and that jig, but none lively enough came to mind. Fionn felt a tap on his shoulder and turned around to see Shayla, Ned and the Kennedy Céilí Dancers smiling at them. He looked heavenward and mouthed, "Thank ye, Jesus!"

"Shayla! How grand to see yez. Right then, will ye want to be doin' the North Kerry set then?"

"No, that's not how our show works," Ned said. "We start out with small céilí dances and build up to the sets."

"Fine, a two-hand reel, then is it?" They nodded. "OK," Fionn said to the band members, "give us a reel."

Aisling started playing "Pigeon on the Gate" and Ned and Shayla took to the floor. They were a pleasure to watch, Fionn thought, especially after the horrors of the last half hour or so. Shayla had a definite feel for the music, even though she had the totally taciturn Ned for her partner. Fionn looked up and saw off-duty Officer Mulroney with a pint in hand, watching his wife with pride. Fionn winked and nodded at him and Jerry raised his pint and gave him a thumbs up.

Another woman from the Kennedy dancers joined them for a three-hand reel next, followed by the four ladies dancing the hornpipe to "The Boys of Bluehill." The four gents countered with a jig to "The Humours of Ballyloughlin." They followed up with the High Cauled Cap, Sweets of May and Haymakers Jig.

Fionn wasn't very happy that their show had morphed into the accompaniment for others, but he was so bloody tired at this point that he had no fight in him and just wanted to get the money from Paulie so they could pay for their car repairs. At least they were playin' the traditional tunes now.

Ned gestured to Fionn that he wanted to use the microphone to introduce the North Kerry Set. As he droned on about the traditions of set dancing, the audience looked about as enthused as high school jocks in geometry class. He was losing them, Fionn could see, and he'd have to get Ned to shut up or they'd start walking out. But how?

Lucky for Fionn, Shayla had showmanship. She walked over saucily and grabbed the mic right out of Ned's hands.

"They don't need a history lesson, Ned," she said with a wink toward the audience. "They just want to see us dance. Am I right?" The crowd applauded wildly, much to Ned's chagrin, and the dancers lined up for the first figure. Unlike Fionn, Diarmuid *was* appreciating their role this evening as accompaniment, because it allowed them to perform on autopilot and get paid for it. This gig had none of the pressure in it that he had with his other band as a warmup act for Christy Moore in Thurles just a year ago. Oh how us mighty have fallen, he mused as he watched the spotlight make Ned's sweaty mustache shimmer. Last year it was St. Paddy's with Christy, this year it's St. Patty's with Paulie.

The children who had been lords of the dance floor before the Kennedys took the stage were miffed by their displacement. So they created their own dance space right in front of the doors to the banquet hall's kitchen. Every time a waiter came out with a serving tray of hot rigatoni or potatoes, they'd almost whack a child on the head with it. Aisling kept an eye on the daredevil dancers and that's why she never saw the guy with Celtic tattoo sleeves, McIntyre kilt, scian-stuffed socks and steel-toed work boots run up and tap her on the shoulder.

"Wanna dance?" he yelled.

Aisling shot a look of fear toward Diarmuid, making him lose the strum for the polka rhythm they were playing for the fourth figure of the set. Neither knew what to do, but Aisling could tell by the meaty hand the tattooed guy held out to her, that she had no choice. She slipped off the straps of her button accordion and set it down on the floor. Diarmuid watched wide-eyed as the beefy guy polka danced Aisling around the entire room. He was furious. He wanted to throw his guitar down, jump up, break a beer bottle and chase after the kilted "King Kong" who peeled away with his girl.

Meanwhile, the college girls snuck into the banquet room and tiptoed around the other side behind Peadar. They ran up and stuck a bobbing shamrock headband on his head with lights that raced round and round. Peadar of course had to keep playing, especially because Paulie was now in the front row sitting with his niece Concetta, watching them carefully. When Paulie got up to head into the kitchen for something, the girls seized the moment *and* Peadar, dragging him and his pipes away toward the bar again. Diarmuid tried to get Fionn's attention at what had just happened to the two other band members, but Fionn was somewhere in the trad moment, eyes closed, playing this polka as if he were performing live on the RTÉ.

Out of nowhere, two border collies zipped through the

crowd that had gathered around the Kennedy Céilí Dancers as they performed, parting the audience like a flock of dumb sheep. They ran full tilt at Diarmuid, who noticed them leaping at him at the split second before they reached his pant legs, sending him scurrying around the room to shake the red and black dogs. Diarmuid zipped around the dancing children and when a waiter came out of the kitchen, he darted inside as the door closed, blocking the dogs' entry.

Diarmuid staggered over to a stool in the corner and sat down, guitar still around his neck. What the feck just happened, he thought. How'd those dogs get in the restaurant anyway? Then he remembered Aisling being spirited away and wondered if this was somehow one of her visions coming true. Instead of coyotes, there were rabid border collies and a tattooed bear on the loose, bent on destroying them all.

Uh-oh. Diarmuid recalled where he'd seen those two border collies before. They belonged to that druidess Danu! That meant she must be in this building somehow. Jaysus, Mary and Joseph, she'd managed to separate the band, too. Was she going to drug them all again and bring them back to her hilltop den of evil, he wondered. What the feck should I do? A waiter came into the kitchen carrying an empty cabbage serving tray and the two dogs scooted between his legs toward Diarmuid sitting on the stool.

"Get away from me, ye heathen feckers!" Diarmuid yelled as he slung his guitar onto his back and grabbed some empty saucepans to threaten them. The dogs snarled and pawed at the linoleum. Diarmuid looked around the room to see where he should make his next move. "Go on, go back to yer feckin' druidess!" he snarled back at them. Another waiter carried in an empty rigatoni tray and Diarmuid bolted out the door just in time to hear Fionn starting the hornpipe for the final figure of the North Kerry set. He set the saucepans by his feet and picked up the tune on the second measure, looking around for any sign of that druidess Danu.

There was a terrible racket of something crashing onto the kitchen floor. It sounded like a wall of glassware and an entire cupboard of pots and pans had fallen at the same time. The door opened but no one walked out. When Diarmuid noticed that, he thought maybe a ghost conjured up by that druidess was on the loose. Of course though, because of all the audience members in his line of view, he couldn't see that the dogs had pushed open the door and scattered the children, whose shrieking caught his attention finally.

"Jayz, they're after me again!" he yelled as he slung the guitar on his back again, grabbed the pots and used them to keep the snarling dogs at bay.

It was odd that Fionn didn't seem to be noticing what was going on. Perhaps it was because every time he looked up, the spotlight was shining right toward his eyes. When he looked away, all he could see was darkness, so it was easier for him to fiddle with his eyes closed. Somehow it helped his concentration. The bright light reminded him of his dream about Annemarie in the jungles of Central America. He felt as if he was surrounded by her shiny gold hair. It made him smile. This one's for ye, luv, he thought.

Fionn's playing had never been better. If only his mates back at the family pub in Clare could hear him at this moment. If only his Da could be there, too. He'd been after him to quit the music and get a job at the quarry with him. Sure it would be steady work and decent pay, but at what price, Fionn thought. His Da's back was wrecked by years of hard labor and he'd lost the thumb of his right hand trying to repair a stone crusher. Fionn couldn't put his hands—the source of his livelihood—in harm's way like that. This moment proved why he shouldn't. His bowing tonight was absolutely brilliant. Och, this must be what heaven feels like, Fionn thought as he smiled. He pictured himself finally winning that All-Ireland Fiddle title, the one that eluded him three times.

He was deep in that trad zone now, playing so sweetly, so effortlessly. Something magical was happening, he had no idea what "switch" had been turned on, but years and years of playing were gelling into musical brilliance right there before his ears.

At the very moment he thought that, he heard what sounded like harp music accompanying him. He tried to open his eyes and look around but the spotlight burned when he lifted them open just the slightest. Maybe he'd died and *was* on his way to heaven, he thought. The harp music grew even louder, as if the harpist was sitting right next to him. He turned his head and tried to open his eyes again, wondering what this paradise looked like, but the fire-hot light made it impossible.

Fionn didn't realize it, but his hearing had become selective, too. Although he could hear his own playing and a harp nearby, plus the patter of the dancers as they stomped to the hornpipe, he could not hear the whimpers of Aisling as she danced past with the tattooed man, the yelps of Diarmuid as he dodged the lunging jaws of the border collies or the plaintive cries of "Help!" from Peadar, who was choking under dozens of green Mardi Gras bead strands strung around his neck.

It was as if a spell had been cast over him. As soon as Fionn thought that, and heard the harp being plucked next to his ear, he realized a spell *had* been cast over him. And he suspected it was that sorceress Danu who was behind it. But how could he break it?

As the tattooed man danced Aisling toward the stage, she could see that the druidess was playing her harp next to Fionn and he was totally mesmerized. Aisling knew it was a bad sign that Peadar and Diarmuid were missing. That evil woman was up to no good, but how could she free Fionn?

"Jayz it's hot in here," Aisling said to her burly dance partner. "Let's stop for a drink," she said hopefully.

"Nope. Don't drink," he said gripping her waist tighter.

"Not even one beer?" Aisling said with disbelief.

"Can't," he smirked. "Allergic. Every time I drink, I break out in handcuffs." He rolled his wild eyes, tossed his head back and howled like a coyote. *Jaysus*, was there any way to tame this beast and pry herself away from his death grip?

When they danced past the buffet, Aisling got another idea. There were fried fish filets for those who didn't eat corned beef. If a salmon of knowledge helped Fionn's namesake from Irish mythology, perhaps a fish filet could help break Danu's spell over him. She reached out and grabbed a piece of fish as they polkaed past, then when they neared the dance floor, she was able to direct the tattooed man toward Fionn, making him bump into him. Fionn's mouth opened in shock, because he couldn't see them coming, and Aisling threw the piece of fish in his mouth. It slid down his gullet easily, popping open his eyes and giving him back his power and sense against the evil Danu.

"On behalf of St. Patrick," Fionn said, stopping his playing, "I banish ye to *hell*!"

Just like that, Danu vanished and so did her treacherous dogs. The college girls suddenly lost interest in Peadar, and the tattooed man released Aisling to get back on his motorcycle and ride away. As he burst open the front doors, an icy wind rushed through the banquet room and circled Fionn. He rubbed his shoulder, trying to shake off the sudden chill.

The Kennedy Céilí Dancers bowed after their performance ended abruptly, exited and the band regrouped on the stage.

"Are ye all right," Diarmuid said as he hugged Aisling tightly.

"I think so. How about the rest of yez?"

Peadar smirked. "Ye know, I was kinda gettin' used to all the attention," he said as he took all the Mardi Gras beads off his neck and tossed them toward the children who'd reassembled on the dance floor. They noticed Fionn looked sad.

"What's the matter, lad?" Diarmuid asked.

"It's nothing. It's just ... for a moment there ... me playing. Och, now I realize I was under a spell. It wasn't really me playing so brilliantly."

"Of course it was yer playin' and it was savage," Aisling said, tugging at his sleeve.

"No, it wasn't. 'Twas druidry. There's a good reason why I never won the All-Ireland."

"Hey, c'mon you kids," Paulie snapped as he walked by carrying corned beef to the carving station. "Keep playin'. I'm not paying you to stand around chatting."

The room simmered down. It was too late for more step dancers to show up. Concetta had gone home with a takeout carton of rigatoni and garlic knots. Finally, Fionn thought, we can relax and play traditional music for these folks—music that can stand alone on its own merit. Let's give them the unfiltered stuff, he thought.

"Peadar, why don't ye start us off with some O'Carolan. Then Diarmuid and Aisling, do yer version of that Sharon Shannon tune ye've been messin' with the past few days. I'll finish off this set with the tune me mother loved so well, *"An Raibh Tú Ag An gCarraig."*

The crowd's attitude seemed different. Were they under Danu's powers hours before and they just hadn't realized it? Now they were attentive and appreciative. Jaysus, Fionn thought, this is more like a pub back home. Whole families were sitting and enjoying the good company, music, food and drink. Peadar was playin' brilliantly, Fionn thought. He, too, deserved to be an All-Ireland champ, had he not caught pneumonia the week before he was to compete that year. Och, Fionn wished someone somewhere in the room had been videotaping this. And when Diarmuid and Aisling launched into their set of lively tunes, Fionn realized how beautifully their styles of playing complemented each other. There was an understanding between the two of them, besides their obvious physical chemistry, that lent toward an exquisite weaving of tone on tone. Peadar and Fionn joined them on the last tune in their set and the audience was clapping their hands and tapping their feet along. It was such a grand moment and the applause was what you'd expect in a concert hall, not a pub.

Fionn waited until the room was as quiet as it could be, then started playing the slow air with sad lyrics, "A Raibh Tú Ar An gCarraig." It tells the tale of a man wondering if his true love was at the Mass rock and if she was being subdued. The setting was a flat boulder upon which Mass was said in the days of the Penal Laws when practicing the Catholic faith was forbidden by the English. When sung in a group of people, the second verse, a response, was code. If the singer sang the verse that yes, she wasn't being subdued, it meant that they could attend Mass safely.

Fionn's mind drifted with the notes that floated from his fiddle. He wondered how a day that was supposed to celebrate the life's work of St. Patrick—converting pagan Ireland to Christianity—had morphed into such a freak show in America. He knew the ancestors of many of the revelers there fled Ireland after being forced to celebrate their faith at Mass rocks or in hedgerows. America offered them the freedom to celebrate the faith St. Patrick had given them. How had it changed into a day of drunken debauchery, twisted Irish folklore and a freakish obsession with the color green?

He smiled to himself. Here in this moment it was coming full circle. For his penance, he—a representative of the land of St. Patrick—was giving them back ancestral music that told the real reason for the season. It was still Lent, a time for reflecting on the ultimate gift Jesus gave the world: his own life to pay for its sins. This beautiful tune would restore dignity to the feast day. It would refocus these Americans at least on the true meaning of celebrating St. Patrick's legacy.

His notes were full and silky-toned. His phrasing was more

exquisite than when he was playing under Danu's spell. For a brief moment he turned toward his bandmates, whose faces were filled with looks of admiration for Fionn's playing. They shared a smile. This was the real purpose of that car crash. This was the reason why they had endured a week of St. Patrick's Day hell. Here he was playing a soulful ambassador, spreading the gospel of true traditional Irish music. As he played, he made his music into a prayer of thanks to God, he was so honored to be the messenger of the moment.

A commotion near the banquet hall entrance disrupted his concentration briefly, but he was able to shift his focus away from the drunken revelers and continue the dulcet tones of the tune. He heard another noise. It wasn't quite like a bagpipe, but something was wailing from that direction again. Being the professional musician that he was, Fionn was able to shut out the distraction and continued playing the haunting melody. He let the final note vibrate on his fiddle perhaps longer than was necessary, and held his breath as he took the bow off the fiddle. Fionn opened his eyes for what he anticipated to be the volume of applause you'd expect from U2 fans.

He got an eyeful, all right. Charging through the crowd at him was a black Connemara pony.

"How'd a feckin' pony get in here?" Diarmuid yelled. Women screamed. Chairs scattered.

"Jaysus, it's me nightmare comin' true. Look who the feck's ridin' that pony!" Aisling yelled.

"Holy mother of God!" Peadar said as he clasped his uilleann pipes to his chest.

"Holy shite and onions!" Diarmuid yelled. "Fionn, get out of the feckin' way!"

An awful specter bearing down on him paralyzed Fionn. Then he heard *that* laugh. That horribly grating laughter. That awful lilting to "The Mason's Apron." It could all add up to only one thing. His eyes focused on the pony rider and he shuddered.

"Bloody feckin' hell! It's Paddy MacSeamus!" Fionn jumped out of the way just in time as the pony leapt onto the stage and Paddy slid off.

"Well, well, well." Paddy said, looking at the band. "Look what the horse dragged in. A ha-ha-ha!"

"What the feck are ye doin' here?" Diarmuid asked.

"That bloody pony ran out in front of me van last night as we were drivin' to a gig upstate. We swerved to miss it and ended up in a ditch. Banjaxed the van. Some fella named Butch is having a look at it. How about yerselves?"

They were all speechless. What cruel bit of fate was this that both bands were detoured here by that Connemara pony? And what the feck was it doin' in the middle of upstate New York, anyway?

"What's with yez?" Paddy laughed. "Connemara pony got yer tongues? A ha-ha-ha!"

"Of all the Guinness joints in all the towns in all the world, he walks into mine," Fionn said walking away muttering, hands rolling into fists at his side.

"What, does a little competition frighten ye?" Paddy said with a mocking tone. "This reminds me of the All-Ireland Fiddle Competition, a decade ago, when it was down to yerself and meself. Remember that boyo?"

Fionn stopped walking but didn't turn around. Both of his

hands were still curled tightly. He closed his eyes and imagined one fist knocking Paddy's teeth down his throat, the other hand ripping off his clown-orange permed hair. Aisling saw the wild look in Fionn's eyes. It reminded her of photos she'd seen showing packs of coyotes attacking a wounded animal. She didn't like the looks of this.

"Afraid to go bow to bow with a real fiddler, Fionn?" Paddy said, puffing out his chest. "Come on, ye wanker. Let's have a little fun here. Let's give this audience the chance to decide who's more deserving of the All-Ireland title. What do ye say? Bygones be bygones? I'm givin' ye the chance ye always wanted for revenge...."

Fionn turned around and walked quickly toward Paddy. He poked him in the chest.

"Yer on, ye horse's arse."

Aisling winced while Peadar rubbed his hands together with glee. "Och, if only I were a bettin' man! This will be the stuff of legends."

"Yer right about that, lad," Diarmuid said.

"What are the rules for this playoff?" Aisling asked Paddy.

"I think we should play three tunes. Each one should be a different tempo. One should be the same for both of us. Another should be our own choice. And why don't we let this lovely lady choose tunes from another tempo for us?" He winked at Aisling. She felt instant revulsion.

"Sounds fair to me. Don't ye think we should have some adjudicators, too? Call it *Traditional Idol*."

"Who will be our Simon O'Cowell? I know, that gent there!" Paddy said pointing at Paulie. Oh great, Fionn thought. We'll be judged by how many slices of corned beef are carved on the buffet during our performances."

"All right, then I choose her as our Paula Abdul," Fionn said, pointing at Shayla. She stood up and looked around at the audience, bowing as they applauded politely.

"One more judge to round out this expert panel." Paddy went over to Aisling and took her hand and covered her eyes with it. "Now I'm goin' to spin ye around and when I stop, ye'll point at someone and that person will be our third judge." His hands covering her eyes made her flesh crawl, but Aisling tried to ignore it and said a little prayer that she'd point at someone who favored Fionn.

He cringed as Aisling's pointed finger swashed across the faces in the crowd. He knew the Murphys might be still there. Perhaps Maurice was out there, too. But it was worse than that. When Paddy stopped spinning her around, Aisling was pointing at a familiar face all right. It was Biff, the college student who threw the chair breaking Katelyn O'Malley's window. Of course he was very drunk that night, so maybe he wouldn't recognize him, Fionn hoped. But when Biff walked up to the *Traditional Idol* makeshift judge's table, he pointed at Fionn.

"You're the bastard that nearly got me arrested the other night," Biff snarled at Fionn. Paddy smirked.

"Ah yes, this will be rich. Ah ha-ha-ha."

Fionn considered the tunes he'd like to compete with. Of course he'd select "An Raibh Tú Ar An gCarraig" for his personal choice. He hoped they could agree on a jig as the same song they'd play. Fionn was ready to play "Morrison's Jig," it had been the tune with which he'd lost the competition to Paddy. He'd been practicing it daily thinking that if he ever had the chance to replay it in front of him, he'd be more than ready. The big question was what would Aisling select for her choices, and would he be ready for it?

"OK, then lass," Paddy said with a smirk. "What would ye like us to play? And who will go first?"

"I'd like ye to go first, Paddy. Give us yer version of "The Sweets of May."

Fionn shook his head. What was she doing? This jig was Paddy's signature tune. It also meant that they would not be both playing "Morrison's Jig," a tune he knew so well he could do Cirque du Soleil acrobatics around Paddy's playing.

Paddy winked at her as he stood in front of the judges, fiddle under his neck, arms poised to finger and bow.

"I like to call this one 'The Sweets of Mayhem,'" he said, giving Shayla a bit of a come hither look. She blushed. Biff pumped his fist in the air. "Mayhem! Yeah! *Booyah!*"

Fionn noted that Paddy didn't bother to fine tune his fiddle and the E string was flat. Every time Paddy played the string it felt like fingernails across a chalkboard to Fionn. While he played, Paddy danced a bit, which seemed to draw Shayla's attention away from his shoddy technique to focus on his sevens and threes, Fionn thought. He could tell that Paulie liked Paddy's suave, Sinatra-like style. As for Biff, well ....

The crowd loved it and Paddy basked in the attention, pointing his bow at random people in the crowd and saying, "Thank ye, luv," even if they weren't looking at him or applauding. How could Fionn compete with this Vegas-style shtick?

"OK, Fionn's up," Paddy chirped.

"Fionn, play us 'Scotsman Over the Border,' *le do thoil*." Aisling smiled, knowing he could show his fine skills off with this lively jig. As he played, Shayla wiggled in her seat to the rhythm. Paulie smiled, as he thought, this reminded him of a tarantella. Biff wasn't impressed. He obviously preferred mayhem in all of its forms.

The crowd also responded well to Fionn's performance, but he feared their applause was a bit livelier for Paddy. So possibly, he thought, this round was close with a slight advantage to Paddy. Next, they had to decide on a tune they'd both play that wasn't a jig.

"How about that hornpipe, 'The Shtax?'" Paddy said to Aisling.

"I assume he means 'The Stack of Barley,'" Fionn said to the panel of judges.

"Come on, lad. I can tell she's a dancer," Paddy said pointing at Shayla. "Haven't ye seen the way she's been keepin' time with her feet? Ye call that dance 'The Shtax,' now. Don't ye, luv?" Shayla giggled and nodded her head.

"Right then, 'The Shtax' it is. Since I went first last time, why don't ye have a crack at it first, lad," Paddy said to Fionn.

"Fair play." Fionn picked up his fiddle and played a lyrical, feather-light rendition of the tune. Shayla closed her eyes and pictured herself dancing with Ned to the music. Oh, they'd be sure to win a gold medal at the feis if they were dancing to Fionn's playing. It was just lovely.

Paddy noticed her reaction and knew he had to do something different to sway the other judges. For as light as Fionn's playing was, his was so heavy it felt like steel clogs hitting a concrete floor. Biff started nodding his head to the music and at the end, stuck out his tongue and did the rock 'n' roll devil horns salute.

"Rock on, bro," Biff said to Paddy, who walked past Fionn and grinned. It appeared to be a draw after their two rounds.

"How will we determine who goes first in the final round?" Fionn asked the panel of judges.

"Pick a number between one and 10," Paulie said. "Three," Fionn said. "Seven," added Paddy.

"It was two. The pony rider goes last."

Fionn wasn't happy with this arrangement. He wanted his haunting version of his mother's favorite song to be the last thing the judges and audience heard, but he had to make the best with the luck he'd been dealt. He took a few moments to compose himself. This would be the moment to avenge years of anger at Paddy, who after the All-Ireland went on to steady success while Fionn had struggled most of his career to earn a decent living. It killed him, because he knew he was a much better musician than Paddy MacSeamus. But what Paddy lacked in artistry, he overcame with an overabundance of showmanship. When people left his shows they didn't remember the music, they remembered the fun.

"Are you ready yet, kid? We don't have all night," Paulie said impatiently.

"Yes." He started out ornamenting the notes in such a way as if it sounding like someone keening. It was mournful and beautiful at the same time. Fionn clamped his eyes shut as he brought the music inside him, and let it tap into all the emotions he'd been experiencing over the last week. Then he tapped into the still festering wound of his breakup with Renny. It worked. The music flowed so beautifully that it coaxed tears from not only Shayla's eyes, but Paulie's and Biff's, too. When he stopped playing, Paulie gave him a standing ovation.

"Bravo, kid. You're like the Pavarotti of violin."

"Thank ye, Paulie. That means a lot coming from ye."

"Oh Fionn," Shayla gushed, "it made me so sad. I absolutely loved it!"

"Not bad, bro," Biff added with a nod.

Fionn walked over to the band and gave Paddy a smirk that said, beat that, boyo. He noticed that Paddy didn't seem to be rattled by the applause and great reviews. What did he have up his sleeve? What trick would he pull to turn the score to his advantage, like he did at the All-Ireland competition.

On that day many years ago, just before Fionn was to compete, he made a visit to the rest room and when he returned to sit before the adjudicator to play, he didn't notice that the hairs on his bow had been slackened. He took his place in front of the judge and when he bowed the strings the first few notes played were mushy. Fionn was forced to pause, re-tighten the bow and start again—an automatic penalty of two marks. At that moment Fionn recalled that on his way out of the rest room, he'd passed Paddy who gave him one of his usual smirks. It wasn't something he could prove and no one saw anyone go near his bow, but Fionn always suspected it was Paddy's handiwork.

Paddy approached the *Traditional Idol* judges table. "If I may, I'd like to dedicate this tune to this audience tonight. This is a very old tune, a beautiful tune, one that will always make me remember this fine evening spent with ye all."

As soon as he started playing the opening notes of "The Londonderry Air," Fionn grimaced. "Feck all, he's playing them 'Danny Boy!' That shouldn't be allowed. There's no way I can compete with that trite melody. The feckin' bugger!"

Diarmuid nodded. "Unfair advantage, fer sure, and a stroke of brilliance on his part."

All of a sudden, a woman's voice intertwined with the melody. Everyone turned around and saw Concetta had returned and was walking through the door, arms out as she sang the "Danny Boy" lyrics to Paddy as if he were her son.

"And he's feckin' playin' it in G flat," Diarmuid added. "Good thing yer not playin' fer money, 'cause that Paddy just checkmated ye."

"G-feckin' flat? It's inhuman!"

At the end of their duet, Paddy reached out for Concetta's hand and kissed it. She grabbed him and pressed his head to her bosom. Women in the audience sighed. Shayla crossed her hands on her chest and sighed too. Biff's head was down so no one could see the tears streaming down his face.

"OK, I think we know who won tonight." Paulie said as he stood up and faced the audience. He grabbed Paddy's hand that was holding the fiddle and raised it to the sky.

"And because you gave us such a good show, I'm going to give these kids a free dinner," Paulie said as he pointed at Fionn's band, "and give this young man the money I set aside to pay the entertainment. I mean, wasn't that 'Danny Boy' alone was worth every cent?"

"Wait a minute, there," Fionn said as he stood up. "That's not fair to me band. We played all evening for yez. We backed yer dancers. We played more than our allotted time, too, because of the brawl between Irish Elvis and Leppo."

"Listen, kid, do you own this joint?"

"No. But ...."

"No buts, I do! And I decide what I can do with my money. Paddy MacSeamus gets it all, end of story. Go drown your sorrows in the corned beef and rigs."

Aisling was furious and stood up, grabbing Fionn's hand.

"As God is me witness, I will never eat another piece of corned beef again!"

"You kids are pretty ungrateful. I gave you work. I'm givin' you pay, in the form of food. It's all you can eat. Go back for seconds, thirds, fourths!"

Fionn was fuming. If they weren't paid, they couldn't take care of the costly bill for the car repairs. That meant spending even more time in this hell hole!

"I *demand* ye pay us for our music!" Fionn said, approaching the judges table. Biff stood up and pushed the table toward Fionn.

"Are you trying to threaten us, punk?"

"Just yer man here, Paulie. He's the one who hired us, he's the one who should pay us!"

"I don't like your tone."

"I don't like his tone, either," Paulie said as he stood up. "Listen you prissy leprechaun, give it a rest! *Capisce!*"

"*An dtuigeann tú an dóid seo?*" Fionn asked as his fist went flying over the table at Paulie but was checked by Diarmuid who pulled him back away from the table just in time.

"Calm down, Fionn. It's not worth it."

"Not worth it. Not *worth* it? Ye've got to be feckin' kiddin' me. Do ye know how many years I've been in the shadow of that faker over there! *I* should be the All-Ireland champ, not that bastard!"

"I agree with ye, but it's just a title. Everyone back home considers ye a fiddle master and this one a joke," he said pointing at Paddy.

"Who are ye callin' a joke, ye stupid culchie!" Paddy said, lunging at Diarmuid's throat.

Gunshots rang in the hall. People scream-scattered, diving under tables and behind the buffet for protection. Diarmuid, Fionn and Paddy looked across the room at a guy wearing a military-like camouflage outfit pointing a shotgun in their direction.

"Who the feck is that?" Paddy said, holding Diarmuid's collar as he pulled him around to offer some protection in case this lunatic fired again.

"Let go of that man," the guy said through the black wool mask covering most of his face. "What's the problem dude, hard of hearing?" Paddy released Diarmuid and backed away slowly.

"Happy St. Paddy's Day," the masked man said as he walked up close to Diarmuid. Something about him was familiar.

"Do I know ye?" Diarmuid asked.

"Yes. Remember? Happy St. *PADDY's* Day."

"Mick? Is that ye under there?"

"Shhh, you'll blow my cover," he whispered to him.

"What the feck are ye doin'?"

"I'm on a mission. Workin' for the IRA now."

"The IRA? They're really here?"

Mick nodded, as he pointed his shotgun toward the rest of the room, moving slowly back and forth. "I met them after the parade. They told me that it was my duty to round up all the English people I met today and lock them up in Vern Warner's barn. So, do you know if there are any English hiding in here?"

Diarmuid grinned as he pointed at Paddy.

"He's the leader of the English Society of Sworn Irish Haters & Puppy Killers. Lock him up first."

"The leader? Wow, wait 'til them IRA fellas hear this. Might score me a promotion." Mick took a pair of handcuffs off his belt and slipped them onto Paddy's wrists. "Come on, you bloody *Sasanach*!"

Diarmuid looked quizzically at Mick. "Wait a minute. Where did ye learn that word?"

"*Sasanach*? You know, Englishman? Those IRA guys taught it to me."

The thought occurred to Diarmuid that perhaps Mick had indeed encountered some real IRA members who were hiding in the backwoods of New York. It would be a perfect base of operations, he thought. Diarmuid looked at Paddy. Did he deserve to be taken away to what might possibly be an execution in a muddy field somewhere? Diarmuid looked at Fionn and could see he was still hurting from the damage done to him by losing the All-Ireland title so many years ago.

"Ah, go on," Diarmuid said.

"OK, none of you people move as I take the prisoner out." Mick led Paddy through the crowd, and when he reached the banquet room entrance, Paulie stood up and whistled. His big, bruising cook bounded around the corner, grabbed both Mick and Paddy by the scruffs of their necks and tossed them out on the curb.

Fionn and the band packed up their instruments to leave.

"Hey, the evening's not over. You guys can't stop playing now." Paulie stood there with his hands on his hips, strutting back and forth like a banty rooster. "I've still got customers. Get back up there and keep playing. I need you there for another hour at least."

"Why should we? Yer not planning to pay us."

"Sure I am. Now that the other guy's gone, you're the ones who will get all the money. You know, by default."

"Sorry, lad. But we're no one's default band. Ye'll pay us for what we agreed upon through Dante or else we're leaving."

Paulie looked around and saw there were still customers coming through the door.

"OK. A deal. But no more shenanigans, OK?"

It was pretty mellow crowd by this point. The children fell asleep in their chairs at the tables. The college kids had left to hit some bars on the way back to campus. Shayla and the rest of the Kennedy Céilí Dancers headed for home. Danu the druidess was gone. There was no sign of the Murphys. There was nothing else left to distract from what was left of their gig.

Or so they thought.

Suddenly, the large HD TVs in the four corners of the hall flickered on. Each one was carrying a different conference in the NCAA Men's Basketball tournament. You see, nothing could top the madness surrounding 3/17, March's "high holy day," except the other March Madness. They'd pared down the field of college basketball teams from the Sweet Sixteen to the Elite Eight. After tonight, it would be on to The Big Dance—The Final Four.

The room filled quickly with burly men shouting at the screens. Workers rolled away the corned beef buffet as waitresses carried in orders of pizzas and wings to newly crowded tables. The green beer still flowed into the room, though.

Fine. Fionn and the band decided to finish the gig they way they wanted to, as if they were at a session in their kitchen back home in Ireland. Just when the music playin' was getting brilliant, a roar would go up in the crowd as a player fouled out or made a three-pointer from center court.

Fionn began to wonder if anyone was still paying attention to them. Paulie insisted that they play until one in the morning. They counted the minutes and seconds until they were off the clock. No one was sitting in front of them listening to their music anymore. They were background noise that sometimes came to the forefront of Paulie's customers, that is, if they got up to use the rest room or wandered back to the bar to update friends on the game.

The moment the clock struck one a.m., they stopped playing. No one noticed that they were in the middle of a tune.

"Let's pack up, grab our pay and get the feck out of here," Fionn said.

"Where are we headin'?" Peadar asked as he yawned.

It hadn't occurred to Fionn, but since Officer Mulroney was called into work to break up a brawl at a bar on the other side of town and Shayla had gotten a ride home with Ned, they had no transportation back to the Mulroney's house. They weren't even sure if they were welcome to spend another night there.

"She'd let us stay there another night," Aisling said. "I think she really liked our music."

"I don't know, luv," Peadar said as he shook his head. "Did ye see the way she got all red when Fionn and Paulie were screamin' at each other? And then she sees Diarmuid talkin' with our 'IRA' friend Mick. I bet there's a sign on her door now sayin' 'No Irish Need Stop By.'"

"I'm so bloomin' tired." Diarmuid yawned. "Where the feck are we gonna go?"

Fionn absentmindedly patted his jacket, like he used to do years ago when he was a smoker, looking to see which pocket he'd stored his cigarettes in. He felt something in his left top pocket and pulled it out. Fionn grinned.

"Ye don't suppose this GPS system could help us now, do ye?"

As soon as he said the words, the screen on the GPS lit up. Instead of an arrow pointing to their destination, there was a shamrock.

"Turn left and walk 15 feet." Fionn raised his eyebrows and looked in the direction where it told him to go. There was Paulie waiting with an envelope containing their evening's pay.

"That's spooky," Aisling said.

Fionn laughed and turned it off as he walked over to Paulie. When he returned with an envelope stuffed with $20 bills, Fionn nodded toward the exit and they walked outside. The temperature must have dropped forty degrees. They pulled their coats up close around their necks.

"Are we goin' to hail a taxi?" Peadar asked. They all looked at him and laughed. There was no way a cab would be way out here on a night like this.

"Turn on the GPS again. Let's see what it tells us to do." Aisling said. Fionn pulled it out of his jacket and flipped it on. It lit up again with that shamrock.

"Wait a minute. How it is doing that?" Diarmuid asked. "Doesn't it need some source of energy to work? Shouldn't it have a battery or plug into something?"

"Maybe it's solar powered," Peadar chirped. They all stared at him. "What's the matter? I thought that was a plausible answer." The other three pointed at the dark sky. There wasn't even a sliver of moon out. "OK, so maybe I was wrong?"

"Ye think so?" Fionn laughed.

"Turn right, walk 400 yards."

"That's scary," Diarmuid said backing away from Fionn. "No way that evil thing should be working." Aisling turned right and started down the road as the GPS had instructed.

"Where are ye headin'?"

"Ye heard the blasted thing. We're supposed to go this way."

"What if it's possessed, like a Ouija board?" Peadar said, eyes growing wide.

"We'll be more threatening to the coyotes if we stay together in a tight group," Fionn said. That thought made Peadar even more nervous and he shadowed Fionn all the way down to Aisling's side. When Diarmuid caught up with them, the GPS instructed them to turn left and go a half mile.

"Did ye hear that?" Peadar said. "It's like it knew that Diarmuid wasn't with us yet. How could it? Wait, ye don't suppose that there are hidden cameras around us and we're on some sort of TV reality show?"

"Didn't ye say that the night of the crash?" Fionn asked.

"Oh. Right. Guess I did. 'Spose I was right?"

The temperature plummeted below zero as they trudged up hill on a narrow country road lined by a tall pine forest. Any time they heard a branch rustle or an owl hoot, Aisling grabbed hold of the closest man to her. Diarmuid caught on that she was doing this and made sure he was always right next to her.

A fierce wind spit tiny ice pellets in their faces. The ice began to accumulate on the ground making it quite slippery to walk.

At the top of the hill, a tractor trailer from a grocery chain was coming around a bend when a Connemara pony darted suddenly in front of it. The driver slammed the brakes. His back tires locked up on the icy road and the trailer swung around as it skidded down into the culvert. Because of the difference in height and the velocity of the vehicle, the rear door twisted open and boxes fell out onto the highway, bursting open and setting free several hundred pounds of plastic-sealed corned beef that began rolling rapidly down the hill.

They were too far away from the accident to hear the squealing tires, but they did hear an odd squishy sound coming toward them in Doppler fashion that sounded like hissing flat tires.

"What's that on the road up the hill?" Peadar said as he pointed toward the bend.

Fionn squinted. "I don't know, but it looks like a slowly

slithering swarm of something dark, heading right for us."

"Slithering? Is yer snake sense picking up anything, Aisling?"

"Not yet, Diarmuid."

"Does anyone hear singing? I wonder if we're near a home around here?" Diarmuid said.

"It's getting louder," Fionn said.

"What is? That weird squishy sound or the music?"

"Both actually." They stopped moving and tried to discern what was coming at them from both directions.

"Look out!" Peadar yelled, as the Connemara pony galloped past.

"Holy feck! Where did that blasted pony come from?" Diarmuid said.

"It's running away from something," Aisling said. "What's chasing it?"

"Did ye see the marking on the face of that pony?" Peadar said. "A shamrock." He gulped.

"I recognize that voice, singing," Fionn said. "That awful voice coming up the hill."

"What song is that?" Peadar asked. They strained their ears to listen, their frosty breath rising in front of their faces.

"*Holy feck*! It's that awful hure MacSeamus again," Fionn said. "He's singin' that eejit dance song he wrote, 'C-C-C-Céilí!' *Jaysus*, we've gotta get out of here. Let's hide over there in the woods."

They followed him as he jumped over the culvert and scrambled up the bank. Fionn hid behind a large lodgepole pine and they crowded in back of him.

"I hear other voices. They sound familiar, too," Peadar said, looking over Fionn's shoulder at the country road.

"Here they come. Get back everyone," Fionn said.

A conga line of people singing along with Paddy MacSeamus to his dance hit, "C-C-C-Céilí," snaked up the road. They couldn't believe who was with him. There were Brian and Kelli Murphy and their three bratty daughters Katie, Kara and Keera. Right behind them were Helen and Velma from the Daughters of the First Settlers. Maurice danced a jig as he locked arms with Danu and spun her around.

"Jaysus," Peadar whispered. "Will yez look at that. I never would have taken him for druish."

"He was kind of a coyote whisperer, if ye recall," Aisling said.

There was Biff dancing behind Danu, with his hands on her waist, followed by Virgil Keane's wife Nolene, whose hands were on his behind. The college girls who fancied Peadar followed, as did the tattooed man, Irish Elvis and Leppo the Clown.

As they came around the bend, the rounds of corned beef rolled swiftly downhill at them like bowling balls speeding toward pins. But the oddest thing happened when they were struck by the beef. They didn't fall down and get injured. They kept conga-lining on, their eyes glowing fire red in the dark.

"Jaysus, Mary and Joseph! They ... they're ... *céilí zombies!*" Aisling said, a bit too loudly. The zombies turned immediately toward the sound of her voice.

"C-C-C-Céilí, Bootyful céilí, yer the only one that I-I-I

dance for...."

"No. *No!* It can't be!"

"What's the matter Fionn?"

He felt sick to his stomach when he saw the woman with the Amy Winehouse beehive whose arm was intertwined with Paddy's. "It's *her*! Me ex-girlfriend. It's bleedin' *Renny*!"

Aisling screamed and the zombies quickened their pace toward the trees. The GPS system lit up.

"*Turn right, run down the hill 20 feet. Jump on the all-terrain vehicles waiting.*"

"What? Is it serious?" Diarmuid asked.

"*Yes, I'm feckin' serious? Ever get eaten by a céilí zombie? Trust me, it isn't pleasant. Now move yer bloody arses!*"

"Jaysus, where'd these GPSes get such attitude?" Peadar asked as they ran into the forest toward the four ATVs waiting with keys in their ignitions.

They started the four-wheeled vehicles, revved the engines and took off just as the Paddy MacSeamus zombie was reaching out to grab Aisling's hair. Fionn led the way, his ATV's headlights lighting the escape path through the woods. They floored it for about ten minutes before stopping to look around.

"Phew! That was close," Fionn said, idling his ATV as Diarmuid jumped off his to check on Aisling.

"Are ye OK, luv? They didn't take a bite of ye or anything?"

Aisling was shaking, but laughing at the same time. "Do ye suppose we'd taste like corned beef to them?"

Peadar started laughing so hard, he fell off the ATV. That made the others laugh even harder, their voices echoing off the pine-topped ceiling.

"*Watch out!*" Fionn's GPS yelled suddenly.

"I don't feckin' believe it," Diarmuid said, looking behind them. "They've caught up to us. Come on, get back on yer vehicles. We've gotta get out of this place!"

"If it's the last thing we'll ever do...," Fionn muttered as he led his convoy through the woods. The path went deeper and deeper into the forest. They had no sense of direction, no idea what part of town they were near. Butch's repair shop, where their car was sitting, could be 10 feet away or 10 miles away. It didn't matter. All that mattered to them was that they must keep moving, keep away from the céilí zombies, keep alive.

Fionn's ATV started to sputter. Ah feck, what's going to happen now? He glanced down and saw that the gas tank was nearly empty. Soon the other ATVs were making the same noise. They had clearly reached the end of the line. Peadar's stalled then died. Diarmuid's was still sputtering and they thought of climbing on his vehicle like an acrobat troupe. His ATV coughed under the extra weight, moved a few feet and ran out of gas.

"C'mon, we'll have to run for it," Fionn said waving them down the path.

"*Where are ye going to run to? Ye can't hide anymore.*"

"Shut up, GPS. We're tired of yer bad karma." Aisling yelled.

"*Good luck on yer own, then. Over and out.*" The GPS's lights flashed off

"Ye should apologize," Peadar said. "There was no need for yer to be so harsh. The aul thing was only tryin' to help us."

"Yeah, Aisling," Diarmuid teased as he wrapped his arm

around her waist and boldly kissed her. Fionn raised his eyebrows at Peadar.

"C-C-C-Céilí, Bootyful céilí...."

"Shite and onions! We're surrounded," Fionn said as the four pressed their backs together and watched the zombies approaching from every direction.

"What are we going to do? Now we're completely helpless!" Peadar moaned.

"But ye know, we're not. We could say a prayer." Fionn bit his thumbnail for a second. "How about that one St. Patrick wrote? 'May we be blessed with the strength of heaven, the light of the sun, the radiance of the moon, the splendor of fire, the speed of lightning, the swiftness of the wind, the depth of the sea, the stability of the earth, and the firmness of rock. St. Patrick pray for us.'"

"Amen!"

As soon as they finished their prayer, lights flicked through the thick forest. There was a truck nearby, and they heard it shift to low gear, then stop. The headlights lit a bright path right at them, blinding and dispersing the céilí zombies. A tall figure walked toward them with a curved staff in his hand.

"Do ye see what I see," Peadar whispered to the others.

"Holy Mother of Christ," Diarmuid said.

"We must have died and been eaten by those céilí zombies," Aisling said.

"St. Patrick?" Fionn mumbled, stunned by the vision before him.

"Yes, my children. It is I, Patrick, servant of God. As you can see, I've been busy banishing some real snakes in these parts."

"Yes, and we're very grateful," Peadar said, hands still folded from their prayer.

St. Patrick stood before them silent for a moment. Then he stretched out his arms and shook his head. "Sakes alive! You don't recognize me?"

"Yer St. Patrick, all right," Peadar said, beaming as if he was seeing a heavenly visage. "Right down to yer Nike Airs. Hmm, interesting detail. Don't think I would have figured saints to be walking around in Nikes."

"Well the clouds in heaven are very fragile. We have to tread lightly up there." He paused again and put out his arms toward the four of them. "Seriously, you kids don't recognize me?"

That voice was familiar. Fionn couldn't quite place it.

"It's Virgil, Virgil Keane! Remember, that night of the car crash I towed your vehicle. I brought you folks back to my home."

"Huh?" Fionn said. "Why are ye dressed like St. Patrick?"

"Oh, I was on a float in the Syracuse St. Patrick's Day Parade today. Just gettin' back from the festivities. Been looking for you folks for a couple of hours."

"Virgil, I have some kind of bad news for ye," Peadar said out of the side of his mouth. "Yer wife, Nolene? She's a céilí zombie."

"I suspected as much. Well then, come on, get in the truck and I'll give you folks a ride home."

As they walked through the woods behind him, Aisling was musing Virgil's words. A ride home, but where was home? She couldn't remember anymore.

Fionn was mumbling to himself. "Renny and Paddy? She never said that she knew him. Wait, there *was* that Michael Flatley fantasy. Ye know, the two do resemble each other. Do ye think she wanted to make me over into a Paddy? *Jaysus*, when we get back to Ireland I'm goin' to confession for real. I've been sleeping with the devil himself."

They crossed into the clearing by the edge of the road and Peadar gasped. "Saints presarve us! It's a miracle! Our car's all fixed."

"I thought Butch said the part wasn't going to get in until next week," Fionn said to Virgil. He laughed and pointed at the sky above.

"Well, you folks see. I have a few connections up there. Here are your keys. Happy trails, folks."

They opened the car trunk to put their instruments inside and were overjoyed to find their suitcases intact. Fionn slammed it shut and they turned to wave goodbye, but Virgil was gone.

"Did anyone hear his truck drive away?" Peadar asked.

They all shook their heads. A coyote howled from a nearby hilltop. Aisling screamed and jumped in the back seat. Diarmuid crawled in after her. "Don't worry, luv, I'm right here to protect ye." She snuggled into his arms and he kissed her hard. Aisling pulled herself back slowly from his embrace and stared at him for a moment.

"What's the matter, luv? Snake sense again?"

"Ye could say that again. What the feck are we gonna tell Eamon?"

Diarmuid winked at her. "Ye see there were these céilí

zombies and coyotes and...." He tickled her and she howled with laughter. Her voice echoed down the woods. It was answered by another coyote. As soon as he heard it, Peadar hopped in the front passenger seat.

He started talking to no one in particular. "Ye know what I've been thinkin', I bet ye could make a corned beef version of shepherd's pie. And I think them corned beef croquettes would be easy enough to make. Can't wait to get back to Mayo and start the plans for me corned beef take-away. Maybe by next year I'll have me own place," he said as he watched Fionn inspect the car tires. And when I move out from Ma's, I'll write that Katelyn and tell her to come over for a visit, he thought to himself. She was already handy in the kitchen, maybe she'd want to stay in Ireland and help run me take-away. Then we'd get married and the band would play at our reception. Och, it'd be grand.

Fionn stood by the car for a few minutes. He smirked when he imagined Rod Serling's voice say "Submitted for your approval...," somewhere in the distance. He sure was glad to see this St. Paddy's *Twilight Zone* episode end, and he didn't need any mystic seer to tell them they were getting out of this place in the nick of time, either. *Jaysus*, it had been one weird trip but at least he'd be returning home with an important souvenir—the soul of his music, restored.

He stuck his hands into the lower pockets of his jacket and felt a piece of paper. "What the...?" He pulled it out and read it: "*annemariesthe1@puca.net Please e-mail me, Fionn. I'd love to discuss a possible tour of Galway Bay next May.*" Fionn punched his fists in the air and let loose a wide grin. "Absolved!"

He jumped in the car, started it up and made a swift U-turn. As they drove away down the hill, the tires thumped over a squishy lump in the middle of the road. Its expiration date—3/17.

Lexicon

Pronunciation of the main characters' names:
Fionn: Fin
Peadar: PAD-der
Diarmuid: DEER-mutt
Aisling: ASH-leng

Irish phrases & other slang used within this novel:
A haon, a dó, a haon dó trí: A one, a two, a one two three (musician's count off)
Amadán: fool
An dtuigeann tú an dóid seo?: Do you understand this fist?
Aul cratur: old creature
Auld: old
Banjaxed: broken, destroyed
Bodhrán: goat-skin drum used in Irish music
Bótharín: little road
Buíochas le Dia: Thank God
Busking: playing music in the street for spare change
Cabóg: clown
Cailín álainn: beautiful girl
Cailín bocht: poor girl
Cailleach: witch
Capisce: (Italian) Understand?
Céilí: a social including dance, music and fun
Chancer: dodgy character
Chipper: fish & chips stand
Codded: fooled
Coladh marbh: the sleep of death
Craic: good times and conversation
Culchies: derogatory slang for country folk
Cúpla: a couple of
Currach: rowboat of tarred canvas stretched over a wood frame
Daft: crazy
Deadly: really good
Defo: definitely
Eejit: idiot
Fáinne: circle, ring
Feis: a competition of Irish dance, music and language
Fleadh Cheoil na hÉireann: Annual Irish music competition run by Comhaltas Ceoltoirí Éireann

Gardaí: police
Gnarling: snarling
Gob: mouth
Gobshite: idiot
Gobsmacked: awed
Hooley: a boisterous party
Hure: rascal, pain in the arse
H'upyaboya: words of encouragement for something well done
Ifreann: hell
Jacks: bathroom
Knackered: dead tired
Langers: drunk
Latchico: someone untrustworthy, a rogue, mischief maker
Le cúnamh Dé: with God's help
Le do thoil: please
Manky: unclean
Piss-up: drinking binge
Póg mo thóin: kiss me arse
Posh: rich, fancy
Púca: a shapeshifting spirit that often appears as a black horse
RTÉ (Raidió Telefís Éireann): Ireland's national TV and radio broadcasting network
Savage: excellent, fantastic
Seán nós: old style
Slippy: slippery
Suigh síos: sit down
Take-away: take-out food

About the author

Mary Pat Hyland is a writer, teacher of Gaeilge, traditional Irish musician and sean-nós singer. She resides in upstate New York. For the past two decades, she's watched St. Patrick's Day revelry from the viewpoint of the stage.

Trust her, it hasn't been pretty.

Made in the USA
Lexington, KY
12 November 2010